I0719483

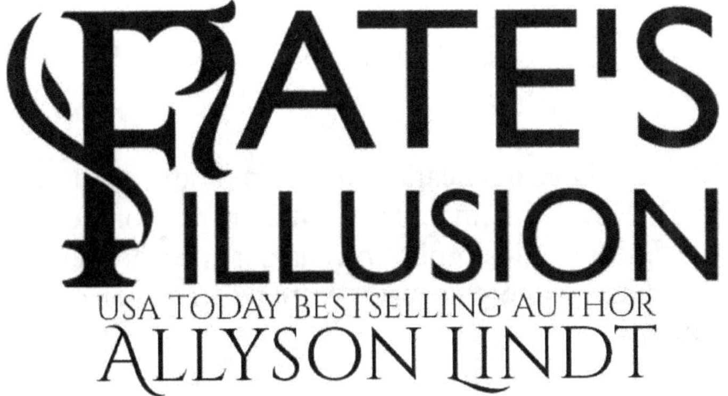
FATE'S
ILLUSION
USA TODAY BESTSELLING AUTHOR
ALLYSON LINDT

Copyright © 2018 by Allyson Lindt
All Rights Reserved
ISBN: 978-1-949986-00-6

Manufactured in the United States of America
Acelette Press

For my eternal dragon

CHAPTER ONE

Lexi learned early in life to keep her observations to herself when she saw someone glowing. Rather than drawing attention by pointing out the faint aura surrounding the occasional person, she looked the other way.

But as she climbed into the cab, and asked the driver, "How much to get to Third and Broadway?" she couldn't ignore the silvery ice he radiated.

"I take gold." He glanced in the rear-view mirror. His gaze met hers in a brief glance, his eyes' intensity and color a few shades darker than his aura stealing her thoughts. If he wasn't bathed in ethereal light, he'd be handsome. Gorgeous.

She dug through the secret pocket of her bag, where she kept trinkets for barter. Praise Aphrodite that she still had this on her.

Lexi's most recent memory was realizing she was standing on a sidewalk in the middle of New York. She didn't know why she was here, instead of in New Orleans.

Figuring out how she got here was critical, but getting off the streets, in case the cameras had identified her, was a higher priority. Cerberus had her memorize a list of safe houses, just in case, and she hoped the one here was still—well—safe. Fortunately for her, the cab she waved down had the familiar pyramid with an eye in the middle on its back window. It meant the driver dealt in barter, rather than digital currency.

A tarnished locket slipped from her stack of cheap jewelry, and a pang ached in her chest.

"That'll work," the driver said. She looked up to see him watching her on the screen in his dashboard that was attached to a fish-eye lens recording the back seat. According to the license displayed on his seat, his name was Actaeon. The glow meant he was most likely a hero—the child of a mortal and either a god or another hero—and the Greek name was probably a tribute to Olympian side of his bloodline.

"It's not up for offer." No way was she parting with the last physical reminder she had of Mom. She shook her head and tucked her mother's locket into the hidden pouch sewn inside her jeans. To him it would look like she stuck it in her waistband. She grabbed a money-clip instead and held it up. "This?"

He shrugged. "Sure."

She set the gold in the lock box between them. It was a simple mechanical device that wouldn't release payment until they both pressed the switch, presumably when he delivered her to her destination. Going digital on something like this, requiring a thumbprint or biometric, would defeat the desire for anonymity that came with barter transactions.

She settled in her seat, and he wove through the congested traffic with the ease of someone who'd been driving in New York a long time.

The air was heavy tonight, the kind most people wouldn't be able to name, if they even recognized it, but for her the excess power sank into her bones and put her on edge. It added to the missing piece of her memory and the fuzzy chunk of nothing in her mind that made her head throb every time she jabbed at it.

"I like your tattoo." His conversational tone jarred her from her musing.

Her hand flew to the mark on the left side of her neck, out of instinct. "Thanks."

Flickers of his glow licked her senses, clashing and mingling with the suffocating night. She didn't know if his presence made things better or worse.

"Why Death?" he asked.

The question cranked her attention another notch. "I'm sorry; I don't understand." It was a misleading statement. What she didn't get was how he recognized the symbol. When she sent the image to Cerberus, he told her it was the mark of her biological father, Hades. He was listed in *The History of the Gods*—required elementary school reading— as dead, so little was known about him. She wouldn't have marked herself with a god if she'd known beforehand. Typically she wore an illusion to hide it.

"Never mind." The shake of his head was slight.

A new weight pressed on her. She pushed his disconcerting question aside and turned her attention to the city. She caught a yellow glow out of the corner of her eye and jerked her head toward the rooftops. The light was different from street lamps, and her gut twisted with recognition before she found the source. *Gargoyles.*

One sat atop a building three blocks down, and another across the street. Two more were within her line of sight. More than she'd expect on a regular night. The cameras kept watch most of the time, but some of the gods didn't trust technology and relied on their own servants as a back-up.

"Is there something going on in the city tonight?" she asked Actaeon.

"Summer Solstice."

Fuck. Summer Solstice wasn't for two weeks. Why was she missing the last two weeks of her life? Acid churned in her gut. "Who's the—" She clamped her mouth shut before she could finish the question. Asking the wrong person who the regional deity was would land her at the god's feet faster than she could blink.

"Poseidon," Actaeon said at the same time her mind provided the answer.

He'd claimed most of the coastal cities. Double fuck. Poseidon couldn't know she was here. He

couldn't know she existed. "Thanks, but that's not—
"

"What you were going to ask. Right. Once again, never mind." Actaeon's cool tone matched his ambient chill.

She needed to phrase her next question more carefully. "Will we get to see Poseidon tonight?"

"Get to?" He snorted. "I assume."

Despite the crowded roads, they were inching closer to the gargoyles too fast for her comfort. If she crossed the invisible perimeter that was their line of sight, she'd stand out in an instant.

She'd need to pick another way to reach the safe house. She pressed her switch on the lock box. "I think I'll walk the rest of the way. Enjoy traffic."

"It's three miles." He took the money clip from its bin.

"I need to stretch my legs before the festivities begin." She hopped from the cab before he could push the conversation.

He'd already turned his gaze back to the road.

She walked in the opposite direction, trying not to be too obvious about looking at the sky every few seconds. If she stuck close to the buildings and ducked down alleys, she could keep a low profile. Gargoyles weren't built to look straight down, and navigating tight spaces didn't work with their wing spans.

One of many things she'd had to learn on her own—Dad's games never taught her that, and the history books tended to leave out those little details.

June heat swirled around her with the movement of the crowds, and humidity filled her lungs. It made it difficult to feel the beasts in the sky, but that meant she was masked as well. Her pulse hammered in her ears, urging her to walk faster.

Another glance behind her, and her heart leaped into her throat at the sight of a gargoyle swooping below the tops of the buildings, in her direction.

The people around her ducked their heads and moved faster. No one wanted to stand in the way of a god's servant, especially one like a gargoyle. No one would help her. She expected that.

She turned down a side street.

The heavy beat of stone wings thrummed in her skull, and the beast swooped in front of her. Okay— not good. It nearly clipped the side of the building. There was no reason for it to risk such a tight space for the average schmuck. But gargoyles supposedly had about as functional a brain as a walnut. If she shifted her aura to act as an illusion, making herself look like someone else, would it give up and go away?

When the gargoyle touched down, the heavy footfall shook the ground, threatening her balance and tentative grip on not freaking out. It growled something. The pitch and cadence might have been words, but not in a language she spoke.

Or, for all Lexi knew, he was just growling.

He stepped forward.

She waved and smiled. "Hey. Got lost on the way to the festival. I figured out where I was, though. I won't keep you." She turned to run from the alley.

The gargoyle was in front of her again, blocking the way out, so quickly she couldn't blink. There were doorways and another outlet, but if it moved this fast, could she get someplace it couldn't, before it caught her?

It would either tear her to shreds or take her to Poseidon. Terror clawed at her thoughts that it might be the latter, and panic surged as the stone monster loomed over her.

The air changed again, washing away the gargoyle's presence and bathing her in a chill. She heard a *zip*, and an arrow of light flew past her. It struck the gargoyle. A shower of sparkles cascaded around the beast, as the arrow vanished, and the gargoyle stopped moving, returned to solid stone.

Lexi whirled, knowing she'd see Actaeon behind her. She didn't expect the blinding silver that surrounded him. As the light faded toward neutral, she got her first good look at him. Pale skin, sculpted arms disappearing into his shirt, and a chiseled jaw. Gods, he was gorgeous. He might as well have been cut from marble. Which meant, in the cab, he'd been cast in illusion too.

A red string ran from his finger to… someplace. Was it some sort of ethereal blood? No. It looked more like actual thread. She'd never seen that before.

She'd also never met an illusion she couldn't see through. Who the fuck was this guy? Not some wimpy half-breed hero, like she originally thought. With the power he radiated, he was as strong as the big names, like—

Her brain stalled, and her head throbbed. Why didn't she remember any of the hero's names?

"It called you a child of Death." His voice sent a chill down her spine.

The gargoyle recognized her. Did it tell Poseidon? Or was he too engrossed in the activities? "So it did say something." She kept the panic from her reply.

"Death has no children."

And it was best people kept believing that. "I thought Death was destroyed by his brothers," she lied. "My dad worked in a comic book store." Her stepdad had—the man who raised her. The person she actually called *Dad*.

"I'd ask how you've survived this long, but you obviously know what to avoid, so…" He turned on his heel and strolled away. "'Night," he called over his shoulder.

Good. If he was going in that direction, she was heading in the opposite. Being near someone with a two-hundred-watt aura was a great way to hide her own, but if he'd been masking himself behind an illusion that still didn't completely hide who he was, she wasn't the only one of them hiding. And he'd killed a servant of Poseidon without breaking a sweat.

She was much better off putting him behind her.

Actaeon headed back to his cab, leaving the woman with the Death tattoo. Stepping in to save someone now and again was fine, but he had to stay off the radar. Not for his safety—he was virtually indestructible—but to keep the mortals around him from becoming collateral damage of one of the gods came for him.

It sucked that leaving her scent behind wasn't as easy. Lilacs and ozone lingered in his sinuses.

Why was he thinking about turning around and asking her questions? There was the morbid fascination that she appeared to be a child of Hades—who was supposed to have died with no offspring. That she might be able to see auras supported that theory, along with that damning smell of ozone. Oh, and there was the fact that she had Persephone's locket, and carried the scent of who he assumed was her mother.

But those were all reasons to get clear of her as far and as fast as possible.

He left the cab behind and walked toward the city center. It was faster. She wouldn't follow. Not after her reaction to the gargoyles.

If she was smart, she'd leave town. If she was lucky, Poseidon would be too wrapped up in solstice activities to notice one little girl out of place in this massive city.

Either way, she wasn't Actaeon's problem.

That didn't stop her from lingering in his mind. It probably had a lot to do with her ebony hair, crystal-blue eyes, and pale skin. Three-thousand-years old, and he still had a hard time ignoring a sexy piece of ass.

Her persistence in his thoughts wasn't related at all to the mysteries she presented. The last several decades had reinforced his determination not to meddle in the affairs of gods.

In the late two-thousand-teens, Poseidon and Zeus decided they'd had enough of begging for table-scraps of faith. They wanted the glory they once had.

They destroyed their brother, Hades, for opposing them—except had they? Actaeon never questioned that before tonight. With the remaining gods, they rose up to remind the people that worshiping them offered more rewards than the technology humanity had put their faith in.

Which struck Actaeon as funny, in a sick and twisted kind of way, because the gods still used the tech. Mostly for surveillance, because their servants couldn't be everywhere, but cameras, digital currency, and other tagged tracking methods could be.

He ordered another beer and downed it too fast. Diving into the past tended to make him drink hard, and meeting Ms. Death weighed on him more heavily than he'd like.

The gods also worked to eliminate or woo any hero or remaining Titan who posed a threat to them. The edict was *pick a side or step aside*. Not the most warm-and-fuzzy marketing campaign ever, but it was catchy.

Heracles sided with his father, Zeus. Atlas had taken his own life after World War II, and didn't have to worry about it. Prometheus was bound in a mental prison. A breakdown caused by something no one had seen, and just as few people knew how to heal. Actaeon's only reason for staying in New York so long was to try to free Prometheus.

Actaeon had tried to stand against the gods, forty years ago. A decade after The Enlightenment.

He tried to take another swig of his drink. *Empty.*

Over the harbor, an array of sparks lit up the night. A century ago, it would have been from fireworks. Tonight, it was Poseidon, impressing his grace upon the people. Reminding them that, as long as they were loyal and offered their faith, they would be rewarded. It was turning their hearts away from the gods that earned them punishment.

Actaeon shook his head. A dick-measuring contest in magic form—that was all the light show was. In Chicago, Moscow, Paris, and São Paulo, it would all be the same show, different asshole behind it.

And if his attitude was creeping into his thoughts that audibly, carried on memories of Las Vegas and what led up to it, it was time to call it a night before he did something heroic. Again.

He returned the cab to the station and hoofed it the couple of miles back to his apartment. The studio was small. It suited his needs, though. It had its own bathroom, and the owner operated on barter. The money clip and others like it wouldn't pay his rent, but a piece from the cache of antiques he owned would do the trick.

He collapsed on top of the bed, turned on the TV to the festivities, and let it play in the background while he fell asleep.

"Actaeon."

The voice jarred him to consciousness, and his eyes flew open. Someone stood in the shadows at the foot of his bed.

"Holy fuck." Actaeon jolted upright, and was summoning his bow before he registered who was creeping in his room. "Pyrcon." Poseidon's left hand.

"Lovely to see you too." The servant stepped into the light of the TV.

Actaeon sighed and leaned his weight against the headboard. "What?" He should have known they had a bead on his location. Hiding from the computer-operated systems? Easy enough. Hiding from the aura-trackers? Not too tough. Achieving both, especially after the stunt he pulled tonight? Almost impossible.

"You killed a stone child," Pyrcon said. He meant the gargoyle.

"It got in my way."

"The encounter happened in an alley."

"Where I have more business than it does." Actaeon would give up as little information as possible. Mostly out of spite. "When Poseidon trains his flying monkeys not to leer at me when I'm getting a blow job, I'll stop killing them for creeping me the fuck out."

"I don't believe you." Pyrcon stared at him.

Actaeon shrugged. "I don't care."

"So you keep insisting. As long as you're in this city, Poseidon is watching you." With that, Pyrcon vanished from the room.

Actaeon needed to talk to Lorelei about another layer of protection. But he'd have to wait until morning, when she was willing to open the gate.

In the meantime, he'd make sure not to help anyone else, and hope Poseidon was too involved with the sacrifices to care about him.

A nagging feeling told him he couldn't shrug this off. This situation was different. *She* was different. Because Death shouldn't have children.

Ignoring the glaringly obvious had kept the people around him alive this long. Why was he tempted to taunt that fate tonight?

CHAPTER TWO

Cerberus stared at his phone in disbelief, before putting the device back to his ear. "Say that again?" Lexi fell off his radar two weeks ago, leaving him in a near-panic and Hades screaming in his head to find her.

"She's in New York." Paul, on the other end of the line, sounded annoyed. He was Cerberus' human connection to the network of cameras and other people-tracking means the gods used to keep an eye on humanity, and his short temper shrank to almost nonexistent when he had to deal with the gods. Those two things made him the perfect person to keep track of Lexi.

Cerberus let a growl slip out, not trying to mask the Doberman-like noise. "What the fuck is she doing in New York?" During solstice. Right under Poseidon's nose.

"Get her out." Hades' command echoed in Cerberus' soul.

That was the plan. He kept the sarcastic thought from his master.

"When she pinged the facial-recognition software, she was getting into a cab," Paul said. "If you mean *why*, I can't help you there. Maybe she needed a ride somewhere."

Holding two conversations at once, one spoken and sarcastic, and one mental, added to Cerberus' ire. At least there was no way that, in all of New York, she'd hopped into Actaeon's cab. The odds of that were one in… well, however many thousands of cabs were in the city.

"How the fuck did she get into a major city, in the middle of solstice, without being spotted?" The question was as much for himself as for Paul.

"This is where she appeared. As far as the tech is concerned, she popped in out of nowhere, though there is some odd feedback on a nearby mic, right before I found her. Seconds later, she got into this cab, and a few blocks after that, she hopped out again and walked in the direction of the safe house."

Cerberus wasn't surprised she'd taken the right steps to hide herself. She was born forty years ago, after Persephone escaped the underworld, pregnant with Hades' baby. Cerberus had been searching for either mother or daughter since, and hadn't found Lexi until about three years ago. She kept a low profile on- and off-line, going so far as to mask her IP and dial in from a different public location each time when she needed internet access.

The only thing that tipped him off that it might be her was her question. She'd been asking around about the meaning of a design she'd found in one of her stepdad's role-playing books, then gotten inked in her twenties. It was Hades' mark, and no copies of it existed online until she uploaded one.

It took Cerberus months of chatting with her just to get her to *begin* to hear him out, and if she had any idea Paul tracked her location over that time, she would have bolted.

"Did she make it to the safe house?" Cerberus asked.

"I'm getting to that part. You want to hear what happens before that, though."

"Kill him and replace him."

Cerberus rolled his eyes. He didn't blame Hades for the urge. "Tell me."

"A gargoyle found her."

"—the fuck? Is she all right? Why in the underworld didn't you open with that?"

"She's fine. The garg is dead."

Cerberus let out a louder growl and clenched his teeth. The phantom sensation of his canine-form's jaws popped in his ears, and the image of shredding something taunted his thoughts. Maybe Paul's favorite laptop.

"She's not that kind of powerful." Not the kind it took to kill a gargoyle. Was she? She could cast basic illusions. She earned spare barter trinkets by enchanting everyday items for people who wanted a temporary change of appearance—hair color, skin tone, and makeup.

But she wasn't a combatant.

"It wasn't her," Paul said.

"When you kill him, make it as slow and painful as this conversation." Hades' suggestion was almost enough to make Cerberus smile.

"I swear to all that's unholy, if you drag this out any longer…" Cerberus left the threat hanging.

"Fine. It was the cab driver."

Right. Because Lexi was so ensnared in fate's web that of course *he* had picked her up. Cerberus didn't have to ask; he knew. "Actaeon."

"Ooh. That has potential." Hades angry tone evaporated.

No. It fucking didn't. Cerberus hated dealing with heroes, but Actaeon… Selfish, arrogant, the son of Artemis and Orion, and the guy didn't even have the dignity to pick a side.

"It's okay." Paul spoke more quickly now, as if he sensed he'd reached the limits of Cerberus' patience. "He shot the beast, said a couple words to her at best, and then walked away. She's in a hotel safehouse, near the shelter."

That was something. "Anything else you want to tell me?"

"No."

"Fantastic. Don't lose her again before I get to her. Check's in the mail. Etcetera, etcetera."

"Right…" Paul never appreciated the old colloquialisms, especially the threat of physical payment. Good. His being irritated was getting off easy.

Not that Cerberus dared do worse. Trustworthy contacts who worked inside the system were impossible to find. He'd put up with attitude and a bit of grief if it kept him in the digital loop. When the gods returned and decided they needed access to technology, to keep people in check, very few were interested in learning it themselves or having their servants do so.

That meant finding humans who were loyal and happy to work for the powers that be, in exchange for a little leeway when it came to how they worshiped. Mostly, keeping their families and other loved ones off the sacrifice lists.

Cerberus disconnected and sank back into his chair. If Lexi had talked to Actaeon at all, he might have an idea who she was. For once, Cerberus was grateful for the hero's lack of allegiance, but if Actaeon stumbled into her, how long before someone else figured out Lexi existed?

For now, she was near Prometheus. The way he bled energy, smothering any other around him, would mask her from any eyes prying for an unusual aura or sniffing out her scent.

Getting her to the labyrinth, to free Cerberus' god, just got a lot more urgent.

It had been more than a decade since Lexi was picky about where she slept. If the bed had clean sheets and a roof over it, she considered herself lucky. Changing her appearance in a restaurant, to look like someone else as she left without paying her bill, was easy. Tricking a hotel that required upfront digital payment? Not so much.

This place, exactly where Cerberus promised, had the tell-tale pyramid on the front door. She'd handed over a gold watch in exchange for a room and now she was settled in to wait out the solstice.

The motel leaked with someone else's aura. The entire block did, so it wasn't as though whoever was responsible had slept *here*. She was pretty sure the heat and grime of ash and smoke came from someone in the homeless shelter across the street. That was where the sensation was strongest.

But it was also non-threatening. Despite the ethereal grit coating her skin, she wasn't scared. And she was grateful she couldn't smell it. Some people could, and if it felt this heavy, she didn't want to imagine what it would do to her other senses.

She knew now why Cerberus told her to come here if she was ever in New York. No one would see her in the midst of whatever that was.

She made herself comfortable at the head of the bed, her back to the wall, and pulled her knees to her chest. Now that she had time to sit and process, she could tumble back into confusion.

Keeping track of dates meant staying alive. So where did her last two weeks go? And how the fuck did she wind up in New York? The only place that would be worse was—

Pain pulsed in her skull as she searched for the city name.

This was so very bad. She was supposed to stay away from somewhere besides here. Zeus' home. And the city name was stuck in the blurry spot in her mind. When she looked in the other direction, she felt fine. *Nothing to see here*, it insisted. *Life is just hectic.* But when she poked to figure out what she'd missed, her head throbbed.

She needed to reach out to Cerberus, but she had to wait until things died down. She'd ensure no one was watching her, make her way to New Jersey, and grab a spare kiosk in an internet cafe. If she flirted with the right guy or gal, she could get them to pay the charge, and no one would be the wiser.

She needed sleep, too. If it didn't clear up the ache behind her eyes, it would at least let her ignore the pain for a few hours.

Poseidon's aura mingled with the one nearby, though. Sea salt under flame and rubble. She couldn't relax while he was nearby.

Lexi grabbed the remote and turned on the TV. The channel didn't matter; they all showed the celebration. This way, she'd look like a loyal worshiper. She couldn't watch it, though. Dad sheltered her from the events when she was growing up, but when she hit her mid-teens, and they were forced to leave behind the sleepy town she called *home*, she discovered Solstice was different for most gods than it was for a spot that offered meek lip-service to Aphrodite.

The first time she saw the sacrifices on TV, she retched for hours after. Individuals could offer themselves up, and Poseidon let them jump into the sea. Ares preferred fights to the death. Typically with bare hands or blunt weapons.

But in every major city it was the same, as the seasons changed. If enough believers didn't present themselves—and there were never enough—families were *allowed* to offer their children or parents up. Neighbors could recommend that guy who mowed his lawn at six in the morning. Depending on the god, either the offeror or the offeree could be taken.

Poseidon liked to let the crowds decide. Felt it made for better television.

She turned up the sound loud enough to be reasonable without annoying the neighbors, and then slipped in her earbuds. Dad's old mp3 player didn't have internet connectivity, so her playlist never changed. She didn't mind. It blocked out the world and let her slip into someone else's.

She grabbed a paperback from her purse and flipped to the napkin marking her spot. Dad loved fantasy and science fiction, but this was a book of her mom's. Lexi'd read it so often, she'd lost count. The man on the cover was shirtless and touched up, so it looked like he glistened in the light.

This book was her favorite. Dad's fantasy novels came too close to reality, but Mom's romance novels… They let Lexi fall into a world where the heroine's biggest worries were securing funding for her flower shop, a kidnapped relative, and whether she loved or hated the rich asshole inexplicably tied to it all.

Lexi could probably recite the book in her sleep, but that wouldn't stop her from reading it again.

A loud knock jarred her awake. She shook her head, trying to clear out the fog of falling asleep reading. Her mp3 player's battery had died. She'd recharge that later.

And there was another knock.

Her heart jumped into her throat, and she crept toward the door. She peered through the peephole, but there was no one in the hallway. She felt them, though.

"Lexi, it's Cerberus."

Sexy voice. She needed to get that book out of her head for now. Sounding hot didn't mean she'd open the door for someone who glowed but wouldn't let her see him. Not that she'd recognize him from his appearance. Online messages were easy to hide. Once pictures were uploaded, they could be tied to cameras. Besides, an aura didn't translate in photos, and that was how *she* identified people.

"I can see you in there," he said. "Violet and pink. Standing on the other side of the door."

"That's the neighbor." She clapped her hand over her mouth.

"Does the neighbor know that rolling a natural twenty is the only way to send me back to the underworld?" A hint of teasing slid into his voice.

She smiled. It wouldn't, really, but Dad taught her otherwise as a child. He'd been around before The Enlightenment, and he'd raised her on pen-and-paper RPGs. In the game, dice were enough to vanquish her foes. No one but Cerberus knew those details about her past, and it had taken him more than a year to earn enough of her trust for her to tell him something so personal.

She opened the door and choked on a gasp when she saw him. Three dog heads overlapped a human one, and paws wavered over his hands. It was like a bad double-exposure photograph. She bit the inside of her cheek, but her whimper still slipped out.

She'd gotten used to most shifters, but their animal forms weren't as distinct as the image she saw of him, and she'd never met a three-headed dog before.

"Are you all right?" Cerberus asked.

She stared at her shoes. "Your illusion is showing."

"I can help with that. Temporarily and longer term, if you let me in."

She stepped aside and locked the door behind him when his feet-paws crossed into the room. Then the human feet were gone.

"You can look now." His voice was in her head and her ears at the same time. It was like hearing through water.

She raised her head, to see a three-headed Doberman sitting on his haunches.

"Is human speech part of the illusion?" she asked.

"It is when I don't have human vocal chords."

"I see." She didn't want to be rude. He was one of her few friends and sources of information. As they built trust in their conversations, he shared that he was a hellhound and servant of Hades, and she explained some of the things she saw—things other people said they didn't. He told her she was seeing through illusions.

She knew from school that heroes had different gifts. The gods liked to fuck, so there were always a couple of their spawn in her grade. But ninety-nine percent of them had gifts like perpetually nice hair or an immunity to all viruses.

If they exhibited any traits at all. A god who mated with another god gave birth to a god. If a god coupled with a mortal, a hero was born. But there was always a chance the child from either pairing would just be human with no power whatsoever.

Persephone was like that. The daughter of two gods, born with no power of her own. She'd absorbed some during her time in the underworld, according to Lexi's dad, and that granted her immortality.

Lexi knew she was different, but Cerberus said she was in the top one percent of the one percent. No one could see through illusions. Not that he'd ever heard of. He also warned her that with shifters it was different than just seeing an aura. She also saw traces of the beast, because that shape lay at the core of their soul.

"I can't imagine what it's like, but I believe you when you say it's startling to see an animal shape overlapping a human one. I know someone who can help you block it out, though," Cerberus said.

Awesome. Fantastic. But something more immediate concerned her. "How did you know where I was?" If he could find her, who else could?

"A friend spotted you when you came into town."

"What?" She lunged for her bag and started packing away her few stray belongings. It wasn't that she'd been seen. "How did this *friend* of yours know it was me?" The answer was pretty clear—someone had a picture of her for reference—but that meant Cerberus had been doing more digging on her than he admitted.

She reached for the doorknob.

"Wait, please."

Instinct told her, *Go. Go now*. An invisible tug prompted her to stay. To hear him out. She summoned her willpower to fight it.

Cerberus moved between her and the door, nudging her back with one head. "Hear me out?"

"How long?" she asked.

"It's hard to say."

"Bullshit. How long have you had a picture of me? How long have you been watching me?"

"Since about three or four months after I found you online." At least he had the grace to sound embarrassed.

She tried to shove him aside. "Then I'd say you've had plenty of time to explain yourself." Frustration leaked into her voice.

He didn't budge. "I couldn't tell you."

She glared. Which head was she supposed to focus on? The one in the middle? That was the one watching her. The other two surveyed the room. It was disconcerting. "Why not?" she asked.

His answer took a heartbeat longer than it should have. "Because if someone besides me is following your activity and they know my guy is watching you, it makes it easier for them to find that same information."

"So maybe you shouldn't have been watching me." She hated that his explanation made sense.

"You know how this works," Cerberus said. "Hades ordered me to keep you safe, regardless of the cost."

"Yeah, yeah. And a servant can't defy the order of their god."

"I'll admit I didn't mind." His tone softened, and he moved aside.

She crossed her arms. A voice in her head screamed, *run, now*, but the tug was back, gluing her feet to the floor and arguing that he made sense. "Really," she said flatly.

"I worry about your safety, regardless of my affiliation. We're friends. Besides, the view is nice."

"Stop." She held up a finger. The flirting was fun and familiar. They'd fallen into it a lot recently, but— "I don't want to hear that while you're a dog. You said you can make it so I can see you in your human form?"

"I can't. But tomorrow I'll take you to someone who will."

She could hang out here long enough to see what that was about, and figure out a new escape plan in the meantime, in case it became necessary. "Fine."

"Are you all right?" His odd in-her-head-but-not talking wasn't as tough to get used to as she thought.

"As good as I ever am. No, that's not quite true. I wish I knew how I got here." The blurry spot in her head pulsed with pain again.

"It's all right. We'll ride out the night, and then visit a place that doesn't reek of brimstone."

"I like it." The sensation of the potent aura had grown on her.

"It's fire."

She studied him. "You're a hellhound."

"There's not literal fire in the underworld. Not like this."

"Oh." She didn't know much about the place, since most things to do with Hades had been stricken from the history books. A yawn crept up on her and overtook her, making her eyes water.

"You should get some sleep while you can. I'll keep a lookout." He nudged her hand with one of his noses, pointing her toward the bed.

She lay down but didn't know how she was going to get comfortable. He hopped up next to her and stretched out. The warmth and strength of the beast by her side was soothing. Something else occurred to her, and she laughed.

"What?" he asked.

"I always wanted a dog when I was growing up. Dad never let me have one. Said it was out of respect for Mom, because she was terrified of them."

"Hmm… Sleep."

She didn't know if that was a good idea, with the pulsating blur of the past couple weeks in her mind. She needed to get out of town, and watch her surroundings until that happened.

CHAPTER THREE

Actaeon felt the warm weight of another person press against him, and his body reacted, his dick hard in an instant, before his mind woke up and registered reality. He opened his eyes, to see Lexi next to him, watching him with clear blue eyes.

Anyone else, and he'd bring up how he didn't appreciate people walking into his place, especially twice in one night.

When her clothes vanished, all of his protests did the same. "I can see through all of it." Her voice was satin against his ear. "That's my gift. Illusions don't deter me."

She could recognize the truth of things? That made her an oracle. Her exposition was odd, but the physical contact made it easy to overlook. He rolled, pinning her underneath him, and locked her wrists above her head. "I'm all talked out tonight."

"No. You're just all talk."

The taunting irritated him, but the way she writhed between his legs, a smirk on her face, made him harder. He glided a hand up her chest, to knead her breast, and languished in her gasps.

Something wasn't right. If she was as turned on as he was, the scent of arousal should be in the air. *Her* scent should be here.

"How did you know who I was, child of the moon?" she asked.

Bloody hell. She hadn't recognized him earlier. Odds were slim she'd figured things out between then and now. His desire evaporated in the half-second it took him to get out of bed. "How the fuck did you get in here, Morpheus?"

Where Lexi had been a heartbeat before, a slender man lounged. Once upon a time, Actaeon had enjoyed Morpheus's lithe, athletic frame. Repeatedly. Over the course of several years.

"Don't stop now." Lexi's voice came from Morpheus's mouth. "Things were getting good."

So the god of sleep had him trapped in a dream. "Let me wake up."

"Don't you want answers first?"

"I don't have questions." Actaeon wanted to climb out his own head, but Morpheus had a strong hold on his subconscious. While they were in here, Morpheus had access to thoughts and desires Actaeon might not even recognize. Though his lust for Lexi didn't surprise him.

"Are you sure?"

If it would get Actaeon out of here, he'd play along. "What will answers cost me?" There was always a price. All the gods dealt in barter, but rarely the monetary kind.

"A kiss," Morpheus sounded like himself again.

Actaeon could do that. Meaningless gestures weren't usually his thing, but he'd make an exception tonight. "Agreed. Who's the girl?"

"Exactly who you think—Hades and Persephone's daughter. And she's going to free Hades."

Ice raced down Actaeon's spine. "Hades is dead."

"Is he?"

Apparently not. "How did you get in here?"

Morpheus crawled toward him on the mattress. "Kiss first, child of the moon."

Actaeon rested his hand on the back of Morpheus's neck and crashed his mouth into that of the god of sleep. The memories of what they had and the betrayal that came after used to ache inside. Now the past was shadows, empty rooms, even in Actaeon's dreams.

"You don't care anymore." Morpheus pulled away with a pout. He couldn't manipulate an emotion within a dream if there was no trace of it.

Actaeon crossed his arms. "You're surprised? How did you get in here?" His siren stone should have kept both visitors out tonight.

"Your stunt with the gargoyle broke Lorelei's spell. You're glowing brighter than a full moon."

"Wait. What?" Actaeon's eyes flew open. He was in his room. The sound of the traffic on the street below filtered up through his window, carrying the oppressive scent of exhaust with it. He could taste the grime in the air.

Yup, this was real life.

Being Artemis' son had gifted him with enhanced physical senses, including that of smell, but unlike the other powerful heroes, he couldn't see a simple aura. But this Lexi woman… She saw through illusions? Was Morpheus telling the truth, or was it a trick to see how Actaeon would react? The way Lexi looked at him last night, after he shot the gargoyle, as though she could see through to his soul, maybe it was true.

But more importantly—Hades was alive. The information rocked in Actaeon's skull. Hades was possibly the most powerful of the three brothers, but supposedly Heracles had killed him.

So much for that. If Hades was enough of a threat that Zeus and Poseidon wanted him out of the picture, freeing him from wherever he was seemed like a bad idea.

And Actaeon would deal with that or ignore it when the time came. First, he needed to see a siren about restoring the spell that kept him hidden.

He'd hoped to pull Prometheus out of his mental prison while he was here, but that would have to wait. Again. He needed to relocate before things got serious. He could ask his mother for asylum, but hiding with her was the same as staying with any other god. It would be seen as taking a side.

He wouldn't cost more lives by sticking around here. The gods might not be able to kill him, but they wouldn't hesitate to destroy hundreds of thousands of people to get to him.

He'd made that mistake once, and it was one time too many.

Cerberus lay next to Lexi, alert while she slept. When she said her mother was terrified of dogs, it gnawed at an ever-present pit in his chest. His job had been to keep Persephone in the underworld, and he always tried his best to temper guard duty with kindness. When she escaped—because he'd intentionally looked the other way—Cerberus suffered Hades' wrath.

Until they discovered Persephone had a daughter. Alexandra.

Cerberus was here on Hades' command, but he had his own motivations as well. He'd keep Lexi safe where he failed her mother. He'd been ordered to bring Lexi to hell and back, literally, but he'd protect her every step of the way.

Nighttime faded from black to gray, and the oppressive scent of sea water ebbed. Poseidon's presence faded further into the background. The festivities must be winding down.

Cerberus nudged Lexi's hand with one nose, to wake her up.

She mumbled and scratched behind his ears.

This was nice. And with the arousal murmuring inside him, quite awkward in his dog form. He'd turn back to his human form when they left here, and with any luck, Lorelei would have a solution for Lexi, so he could stay on two legs more often than not.

"Time to wake up," he said.

She peered at him through half-lidded eyes, sleep lingering in her gaze. She focused on him. "Is Poseidon gone?"

"Soon. You've got time to shower and gather up your things."

She sat, swung her legs over the side of the bed, and kicked a foot in the direction of a leather backpack sitting a few feet away. "That's everything I own. Give me fifteen minutes."

The shift in her tone—the edge of bitter sadness—dug deep. He knew from their conversations that she'd been running since her stepfather died, more than twenty years ago.

Cerberus usually hated online interactions. If he couldn't see a person, smell them, sense their shift in posture or tone, he couldn't read them. With her, he swore hints of emotion carried to him digitally. Perhaps it was blind hope on his part, but he suspected it was more. A stronger bond he couldn't see.

When she vanished into the bathroom, he took the opportunity to shift back to human. It wasn't a physical transformation per se. Both the dog and human forms were shells for his ethereal body, so this was a matter of summoning one and stowing the other in a sort of pocket reality that was only his.

His human shell still wore the clothes from last night. He wriggled his limbs, taking a moment to adjust to the skin, like sliding into a snug sleeve.

Lexi returned a short while later in fresh clothes, her damp hair pulled into a ponytail. The artificial flower scent of hotel soap clung to her skin but didn't hide what lay underneath. "What's the plan?" she asked.

Down to business. He liked that. It would be nice if there were time to chat, like he was used to with her, but that would wait. "We have a few blocks to go, to get to the person who can hopefully help you get a grasp on the seeing through illusions."

"That's convenient, that they're in New York."

He shook his head. "She's in Hawaii. She likes to watch the ships. But there's a spot nearby where ley lines converge, and that's our gateway to her."

"Like a doorway to Narnia?" Lexi sounded skeptical.

"Almost exactly, but it's a in a broom closet, not a wardrobe." The sea salt charge in the air dipped, like a flame being snuffed. This was their window. "I'll fill you in on the rest later. I promise. We need to leave now. If you see *anything* on the way there, let me know."

She nodded. The lack of questions would make this easier, but it made him suspicious too. If she didn't trust him, if she was looking for a chance to run, he needed to be on his guard.

They left the grimy hotel room behind. As they reached street level, Prometheus's scent grew more potent. Without a god to mask it, it dominated the air. It would hide Lexi and Cerberus, but it fucked with his senses as much as anyone's.

The leaking power was what made this nearby trip possible, though.

"What is that?" Lexi asked. "It's stronger over there." She nodded at the shelter.

"Prometheus." Cerberus gestured down the street, and she fell into step beside him.

"As in, gave fire to man, chained to a rock for eternity? That Prometheus?"

"Exactly. Except he broke free of the rock ages ago, and he's trapped in more of a mental prison now."

Lexi glanced at him, mouth quirked. "They don't teach that in the history books." She looked past him, toward the other side of the street. "We need to run." Her body went rigid, and fear seeped into her aura.

He followed her gaze. The streets weren't as packed as they would be midday, but small pockets of people wandered down the sidewalks. None of them stood out. "There's nothing there."

"The woman with the green streaks in her hair, wearing the earbuds? She's a fucking harpy."

A shiver ran down his spine as he picked the face out of the passersby.

She looked directly at him, and her voice echoed in his head. *Hello, brother.*

"Run," he said to Lexi.

Lexi was already sprinting down the sidewalk. Concern for her hammered in his ears and hummed with raw adrenaline through his veins. Once upon a time, Harpies had served Hades, but with his imprisonment, they offered their loyalty to Zeus.

They were vicious hunters, capable of masking their aura and ethereal scent, and if one had orders to snag Lexi, they'd torture her first, just for fun.

He wanted to run at a full-out gallop. To yank Lexi along. He wouldn't leave her behind, and apparently she ran like a human.

If the harpy was in human form, she wasn't supposed to draw attention. That was a plus, but it meant Zeus knew Cerberus and Lexi were here.

Cerberus' bare feet slapped against the pavement, in time with his heart. He was glad he'd left the shoes behind. He urged Lexi toward a more crowded part of the city. It was on their way, and he hoped the people would slow down a harpy supposed to keep a low profile.

Come back, brother. I only want to talk, the harpy said in his head.

Fuck you. He forced mental blocks into place, to keep her from speaking to him telepathically.

A glance over his shoulder told him she was closing in, and Lexi was lagging behind. They were so close to their destination.

"What's that feeling?" Lexi asked between gasps for air.

"Convergence point." He yanked her into the coffee shop.

A few people sat at the tables, and a couple more stood in line—the remnants of late-night revelers and a hint of early-morning commuters. He shoved past a couple in the middle of the store, knocking them aside.

"Sorry," Lexi called at them over her shoulder.

If she was this soft, it could be a liability. He looked back to urge her to hurry.

The harpy grabbed Lexi's shirt.

Cerberus shifted in a blink and bit down on the bird-lady's arm. He nodded toward the broom closet with another head. "Through that door. Keep running. Don't look back."

Lexi nodded.

Cerberus sank the jaws of his third head into the harpy's throat, and she let out a horrific screech. It stopped as the taste of blood blossomed over his tongue, stinging his senses.

He was vaguely aware of the people around him backing up. Looking the other way. Offering audible vows that they weren't a party to this.

He snapped his jaw until he was certain the harpy was dead, then tore away. Zeus would send someone else immediately. They needed to get out of here.

Cerberus rushed into the closet. The back wall had given way to a gorgeous beach. Lexi hadn't gone through, though. She leaned against a nearby shelf, a hand pressed to her forehead, her skin pale. Her breath came in short gasps.

He didn't know what was wrong, but there was no time to find out. He grabbed her arm with his teeth—far more gently than he had the harpy's—and yanked her through the ethereal doorway. If gods answered prayers, he'd send one to the closest deity that this trip didn't destroy her.

CHAPTER FOUR

Lexi had so many questions as they stepped through the wall, her eyes squeezed shut because of the pain. Cerberus didn't hesitate to kill for her. Did she owe him something in return? Why was her head pounding so hard she wanted to tear it off? Why was a harpy after her…?

Pretty music. The thought erased everything else. It wasn't quite a song; it was birds on a calm morning, and the rush of water over rocks, and a lullaby. It felt like love, and it left an ache of longing in her chest.

Something nudged her senses, but at the same time it was just out of her grasp. She forced her eyes open, and at the sight of a sharp, vicious aura, stepped back involuntarily.

"Lorelei, she's with me." Cerberus moved in front of her.

Something else mingled with the onslaught of contradiction. Ice. Safety. Protection.

"Actaeon?" Lexi said.

The woman with the jagged aura smiled. "She's exactly what you said." Her voice was lilting and mingled with—rather than disrupting—the song in Lexi's head. Under the violet and yellow that sparked around her like shattered glass, she was beautiful and terrifying.

"It's not the kind of thing I'd lie about." Cerberus's voice was a growl.

Lexi felt out of sorts. Nothing was what she expected. That coldness underneath it all, though... She knew that feeling, though she'd only been exposed to it once. It was frozen in her soul. "Actaeon?" she asked again. If he was here, she didn't want to be. Any guy who could take down a gargoyle with an invisible bow was a beacon she didn't care to stand near.

So why did she want to find him? To talk to him?

The woman—Lorelei—gave her a tired smile. "I don't discuss my clients with anyone. You can see me?"

Lexi nodded. "Where's the music coming from?"

"I'm a siren, love. I *am* the music. And you can't see past it with your eyes closed."

Odd statement. "So?"

"Cerberus told me you see things no one else does. If the music hides me, it means I can help you."

"Why would you do that?" Lexi had a feeling this woman didn't want a gold watch as payment for services rendered.

"Because I'll pay her. Very well," Cerberus said.

Lexi clenched her jaw. "What will it cost *me*?" First saving her life, and now whatever this was? Talking to Cerberus over the internet was one thing, but these were some serious favors.

He looked at Lorelei. "Give us a few minutes?"

"You know where to find me." The siren turned and headed into a small cottage a few hundred feet from the water.

Could Lexi get out of here? She didn't think she could swim to a safe location. Especially not through the ocean. If harpies were looking for her, did Poseidon have other creatures out there too? She'd never seen a merman…

She didn't want to. The books painted them as vicious and vindictive.

"It won't cost you anything." Cerberus sounded sincere.

"Why not? Where are we? Are we safe here?" Those were the important questions. The others would wait for a heartbeat, until she had her first round of answers.

"Because I serve your father, and I serve you. No payment is required. We're in Hawaii, like I promised. And we're safer here than most places."

She only half-heard his last two answers. The first caught in her chest and squeezed. He said the words with such conviction. Servants swore complete and unyielding loyalty to a god. But she'd never witnessed it.

She had a hard time trusting that anyone she bought a sandwich from wouldn't spit in her food. Cerberus gave Hades *everything*. She tried to wrap her brain around it, even with it being right in front of her. She let the notion roll in her head and moved on to his other replies. "*Safer here than most places* isn't reassuring."

"Lorelei wraps her island in music. It's an aural illusion instead of a visual one, and it means what's on the inside stays inside, and the rest stays out. She gets away with not swearing loyalty to a single god, because she helps all of them. In return, her island is neutral territory."

"Did you really kill that harpy?" Lexi only saw hints of blood before she rushed into the closet, but it was enough to give her an idea.

"It was her or you. How do you need me to phrase it, so you understand your life is my priority?" Cerberus rested a hand-paw on her cheek. Comfort flowed through the touch. Loyalty. Trust.

All bad things to let herself feel. She couldn't afford to drop her defenses to anyone.

She broke the contact, and regret washed over her. "You'll forgive me if it takes a little time to get on board with that. It's not quite in sync with the rest of my life."

"I understand." He gestured toward the hut. "Are you willing to talk to Lorelei?"

"If she tries to kill me, will you rescue me?"

Cerberus nodded. "She won't. But yes."

"Then I'll see her." Lexi kept her suspicion near the surface and followed him inside. The music was louder in here, soothing her soul and chasing away her reservations. Making it hard to hold onto skepticism.

Lexi wanted to fall into the song and let it wrap around her. It wouldn't hurt to do so for a little bit, would it?

Actaeon stepped into the room through a door across from them. The cool helped wake her up, but not enough.

Cerberus growled—a low, disquieting sound that rumbled over her.

"Are you everywhere?" Lexi asked.

Actaeon's gaze was locked on her. Why? "I'm where I need to be, to fix what you broke."

She didn't appreciate the accusation. "I didn't break anything. I got in a cab and out again. The rest was on you."

"Hey, pup." Actaeon looked past her. "Daddy send you to watch the kid?"

The sound rolling from Cerberus's chest grew in volume.

"Gentlemen." Lorelei's voice was sharp. "Do I need to remind you of the rules?" She smiled at Lexi. "No killing on my property."

Because of course that was a rule. But it was another thing Cerberus was honest with Lexi about, and she liked being able to believe the things he said.

Actaeon crossed the room. When he grasped her fingertips, a jolt raced through her. He raised her hand and drew his nose along the inside of her wrist. A pleasant shiver raced over her skin, and she parted her lips in a silent sigh. *More, please. His mouth on her neck... His hands gliding along her bare torso... Energy sliding between them...*

"Let go." Cerberus's low and threatening bark jarred Lexi from her downward slope of desire.

She said, "Down boy," at the same time Actaeon did. A laugh slipped out without her permission.

Actaeon dropped her hand. "I thought Persephone was dead."

"She is." Lexi frowned. "She died shortly after I was born."

"I'm sorry." Actaeon sounded sincere. "She was a wonderful person, every time I spoke with her. She never deserved her fate."

He knew her mother? A million more questions surged forward in her mind, carried on a wave of grief.

"This is lovely." Lorelei's sweet voice cut through it all, silencing Lexi's thoughts. "Whatever it is. But you're on my clock, and you don't want to run into my next appointment." She looked at Lexi and nodded at Actaeon. "What do you see when you look at him?"

The marble statue who'd saved her was gone, replaced by the cab driver encased in ice. "A guy. Kind of cold. Pale-white aura. Conflict. Ambivalence. Obligation. Loathing. Duty—"

"Enough." Actaeon's sharp tone silenced her.

"What did you see last time you met him?" Lorelei asked.

"It was like one of those Michelangelo statues. Carved marble, bathed in moonlight."

Actaeon shook his head. "Your oracle is broken."

Lexi clenched her jaw. He made it easy to forget she was fantasizing about him moments earlier.

"I think she works fine. You're done. Keep the heroics to a minimum, because I'll charge double if you're back here in under a month." Lorelei pointed Actaeon toward the door.

"I plan to stop them altogether." Actaeon didn't budge.

Lorelei extended her hand to Lexi. "Come with me."

When Lexi grasped her fingers, she expected a shock of *something*. Instead, it was simply skin on skin.

"My magic is in the music." Lorelei led her through the door Actaeon had come out of.

The walls were draped with layers of soft, translucent fabric, giving the room an almost hazy feeling. Pillows lined the floor and the benches that ran along the edges. That desire to lie down and nap was back. Lexi kept it at bay by focusing on the siren. "What kind of payment do you take?" She half-believed Cerberus had it under control, but asking seemed important to cementing reality.

Lorelei's smile chilled Lexi and churned in her gut. "It all depends on the client," Lorelei said. "The right hero has a lot more to offer than a servant. I do so hope Actaeon comes back soon."

New images licked the edges of Lexi's thoughts. A grotesque series of stills—either pleasure or pain. Possibly both.

"Let's get you some solid footing." Lorelei turned to a jeweled box sitting near a bureau mirror. Her reflection was gorgeous. Flowing ebony hair and porcelain skin. Mirrors hid the truth from Lexi as much as cameras did. They only captured the physical, not the ethereal.

Lorelei turned back around and held out an earring clasped between her thumb and forefinger. "Let's give this one a try." She held it near Lexi's ear.

The sharp pain from the cafe was back, and Lexi gasped as it rocked in her skull. It intensified until her vision wavered, and she thought she might faint.

"Interesting." Lorelei moved her hand away, and the headache vanished. "That won't do at all. Where have you been recently?"

"A hotel room in downtown New York." No reason to lie about that. It seemed everyone knew.

"Before then?"

Lexi poked the edges of her mind, colliding with that fuzz of uncertainty again. "I don't know." It was the answer she'd give anyway, but it bothered her that she really didn't.

"Fair enough." The siren returned to her jewelry box. When she spun toward Lexi again, she held a different earring. A sparkling red gem on a golden cuff. She moved it close to Lexi's head, and Lexi braced herself for more agony.

Instead, the shattered glass aura around Lorelei faded, leaving her looking like her reflection. A low, pleasant hum rolled through Lexi's head.

"What do you see?" Lorelei asked.

"You. But not. I see the lie." Lexi clamped her mouth shut. That probably wasn't the best way to phrase her response.

"Perfect." Lorelei grabbed an odd-looking device from her dressing table, like a plastic craft gun, and fitted the earring into it. She scooted closer to Lexi and reached for her ear with the device.

"Whoa. What are you doing?" Lexi stepped out of her grasp.

"It's an earring. You're getting a new piercing."

"Why?"

Lorelei pursed her lips. "Did Cerberus tell you anything?"

"That your music was its own illusion, and you could help me control the things I saw."

Lorelei held up the ear cuff again. "This has traces of my magic attached to it. It acts a lot like any music player, but it's tuned to your frequency. When the music hums from it, only you hear it, but it will imply that you ignore the things you've been seeing."

"Oh. Is that all there is to it?" It sounded similar to the charms Lexi sold, except hers were one-time use, only meant to last a few hours, and didn't impact her. "And you're going to just give it to me?"

"We covered that. Cerberus paid before you arrived. He'd do pretty much anything for you."

Lexi was starting to believe that he believed it. "All right. Pierce me."

Lorelei leaned in again, clamped the piercing gun in place, and a pinch later, pulled away. "Reach your finger up there."

Lexi did.

"One tap will turn it on."

Lexi tapped the gem, and the faint music drifted toward her again. It was more of a suggestion of a song, than an actual melody. Once more, Lorelei's aura vanished, leaving a stunning porcelain-doll-like woman across from Lexi.

"Two taps are off."

Lexi tried it, and the world returned to the one she was used to. This would take some adjustment. She turned the earring back on. "Thank you."

"I'd say it was my pleasure, but… No, wait—it was. Your guardian is a beast of a servant." Lorelei gestured toward the door.

The words churned in Lexi's gut, and her mind refused to ignore the implication this time. She didn't care what other people did with their time—to each their own, even if that meant swapping sex for favors—but the strobed stills of Cerberus sleeping with Lorelei that flashed in her head were tainted with horror, not passion.

Cerberus didn't do that for her, did he?

Never again.

The fierce thought caught her off guard, but the truth of it seeped into every inch of her, carried on an unexpected surge of jealousy.

She tried to shake it aside and failed.

Cerberus paced the waiting room when Lexi disappeared into Lorelei's office.

Actaeon had settled onto a couch and sat with his arms crossed. Why was he still here?

"Morpheus visited me last night," Actaeon said.

Fuck. That meant Hades was working other angles, in case this thing with Lexi didn't work out. None of the previous plans had, so Cerberus understood. But this time was different. Lexi was actually Hades' child. And a true oracle.

One of a kind, in every way.

51

"Is Hades alive?" Actaeon asked.

"Why do you care?'

"Because the world has enough assholes in it, and if you plan to trick that young lady into loosing another one, I'm going to kill you right now."

A tremor of fear raced through Cerberus, and he squashed it. "You won't touch me." Lorelei wouldn't allow it.

"If *the* siren banished me, it would make one hell of a statement. Don't you think?"

"You won't, because you never do." Cerberus didn't have a problem calling Actaeon's bluff. The child of moonlight valued his reclusion too much, to piss off the siren who helped him hide.

Actaeon shrugged. "Assure me, and we won't have to find out."

"Tell him," Hades said in Cerberus' head.

"He might be a free agent, but that won't stop him from spilling news to someone if he doesn't like what he hears."

"You misunderstood me." Threat wove through Hades' words. *"It's not a request. Tell him."*

"Yes, we're going to free Hades, who is quite alive and imprisoned in the labyrinth," Cerberus said.

Actaeon stood and uncurled his arms. His fingers twitched.

"Let me finish."

"I'm waiting." The light show that flicked over Actaeon implied he wouldn't do so much longer.

"Zeus and Poseidon trapped him in there for a reason. Because he disagreed with this insane idea of rising up and retaking their places in the people's hearts. Hades doesn't want a place on an earthly throne. He wants the gods to go home as much as humanity does, so he can return to the underworld."

"Mighty altruistic of him." Actaeon's voice was flat.

"Not really."

"Oh?" Sarcasm dripped from the simple question.

Cerberus snarled and stood taller. "They trapped him in a maze. Stole his home and killed the woman he's loved for millennia. He's going to publicly eviscerate them, the moment he's free. He's going to exploit this public network of instant news and gratification they feed on, to talk to the public. He's going to ensure the world knows they can be beaten, and make every other god in existence sorry they took him from his life for so long. And once the gods are cowering at the rage and rebellion of the masses they've oppressed for so long, he's going to go home and watch from afar as they suffer."

"Hmm. That does sound like Hades." Actaeon nodded. "How does Lexi make that possible?"

"You said it yourself—she's an oracle. She can see the truth of the illusions that keep Hades trapped in the labyrinth."

"And you'll handle everything that's not an illusion?"

"Yes."

Actaeon snorted and turned away. "Good luck with that." He strode out the door.

"*Recruit the hero.*" Hades' command rolled through Cerberus' thoughts.

"*Not Actaeon. Anyone but him.*" Cerberus was willing to lay his life on the line for Lexi, but he wasn't willing to sacrifice himself before the quest started, by pissing off the wrong guy.

"*Are you refusing me?*"

Hades' rage rolled through his thoughts, and Cerberus gritted his teeth at the onslaught. "*I'm not. He will. We can do this alone.*"

"*If you fail, she won't live,*" Hades said. "*You know that, don't you? Persephone's daughter will die. If that happens and you survive, I'll never let you forget it.*"

Hades had a point. Cerberus didn't know if he could face the trials of the labyrinth with just Lexi. It didn't make it any more likely that Actaeon would help.

He didn't even know where the hero had gone. Almost certainly not back to New York.

Cerberus would have to cross his fingers and hope he had time to prepare Lexi for what lay ahead. Because if she died, Cerberus was capable of doing far worse to himself, guilt-wise, than Hades could in a century.

And Hades wouldn't let death be his escape.

CHAPTER FIVE

Lexi stepped back into Lorelei's waiting room. When her gaze landed on Cerberus, she let out a soft *oh*.

He whirled to face her, and the deep lines in his forehead faded, replaced with a smile. A dark, trimmed beard covered his chin, and his hair was the same color. He had sharp, chiseled features, softened by the way he studied her, his eyes so dark they were almost black. "How are you doing?"

"You're gorgeous." As in, fuckably so. A man who was completely dedicated to protecting her, was stunning, and got her old-school references? Dangerous combination.

His smile grew. "You don't like my dog half?"

"Imagine a series of overlapped images, like a bad double exposure. You were a blur to me before."

"So you're good, then."

She was so far from good, it wasn't funny. She'd spent most of her life hiding from the deities who ruled this world, unable to call any place *home* after Dad died, and she'd never been so not-fine. "I can see you more clearly. *Good* is hoping for a bit much."

"I'm taking you someplace safe. That should help."

She suspected his definition of *safe* was different from hers. "What's wrong with here?" she asked.

"Not all of Lorelei's clients are as *personable* as Actaeon. And while this is a no-fight zone, we don't need another random knowing you're out there."

That was the easiest to accept thing she'd heard in the last twenty-four hours. Lying low was high on her priority list. "Where are we going?"

"Missouri."

Mormons. One of the Christian religions. According to Dad, when The Enlightenment happened, Mormons saw it as a sign of the last days, and called their people back to Missouri. They didn't give their faith to the gods, so no one had power there. Most people never heard of them because, like so many things, they'd been stricken from the history books. According to Dad, it was easier to ignore them and make sure the rest of the world did as well, than fight them.

"*No gods* sounds like my kind of place," Lexi said.

"I'll buy you lunch." Cerberus chuckled.

"What's funny?"

He pointed her toward the door, and they stepped onto the beach. "You'll probably think I'm ridiculous, but I've wanted to say that to you for a while."

There was that hint of flirting again, and when he looked like this, rather than a blurry dog, it was fun to hear. Sand stretched in front of them, colliding with the blue waves of the ocean. They walked toward the water, but had only gone a few feet when a door appeared in front of them. A faint ringing echoed in her ears, and her headache returned, but not nearly as debilitating as before.

They stepped through the door and were in an abandoned lot. As their new surroundings solidified, the pain vanished. "Why does that hurt?" she asked.

Cerberus looked at her, brows furrowed. "What?"

"Whatever we just did."

He shook his head. "I don't know. It's siren magic, but it should be painless." He looked like he was telling the truth.

She'd leave that question on her list and move to the next one. The agony was gone, which meant other things were more pressing. Her stomach growled. "What's for lunch?"

"There." He nodded across the street. "Killer burgers, but really, they're about the cupcakes."

She didn't think she'd ever been in a diner where the specialty was cupcakes, but right now she could eat about fifty. From the outside, the place was another blank face in the middle of a strip mall of *For Lease* buildings. Inside, the scents of grease, meat, and a dozen other flavors she couldn't identify rushed over her.

And there was the distinct absence of auras. It might be because of the earring, but she still felt Cerberus. "It's amazing."

"It gets better." To the hostess, he said, "Booth for two."

The girl looked like she was in her early twenties. Then again, so did Lexi, despite being forty. The waitress handed them menus, took their drink orders, and turned to leave.

Cerberus stopped her. "Two of the house-specialty burgers. Rare on one." He looked at Lexi.

"Medium-well for me," she said.

Cerberus wrinkled his nose. "And extra fries."

The girl left.

"You have questions," he said to Lexi.

"You knew my mother." It wasn't a question, but they weren't allowed to talk about Mom online. Keeping discussion of her parentage to a minimum helped them avoid pinging random filters. "Tell me about her."

Cerberus grabbed the napkin wrapped around his utensils, peeled off the paper tab holding it all together, and folded the paper into tiny squares. "I can tell you a lot more about your real father."

She'd been hearing about the gods all her life. Even if Hades wasn't on the list, she could wait another five minutes to learn more. "Why did Mom leave the underworld? Was she unhappy there? Was she as sweet as Dad said?" She stopped herself before overloaded on the questions.

"I don't know. I don't know. And yes." He looked at her with the last answer.

Disappointment sank inside. He was lying about the first two. So much for getting him to open up.

She was curious about Cerberus' comments regarding Prometheus, but that was on the list of *not pressing issues*. "Why does everyone keep calling me an oracle?" Cerberus had used the word several times, and what she was didn't seem to be a secret. When she'd tried to research it, the only information she found was about women who lived ages ago. "I can't see the future."

"Different oracles have different gifts, but they all share one trait—they see the truth of things. Some see the truth of what's coming, and others recognize the truth of what came before. You see things for what they are now. Or, put more simply, you can see through illusions. Except siren ones, apparently."

"Oh." That made sense. She was trying to decide where to go next, when their food arrived.

Lexi thought she'd adjusted to the mouth-watering smell, but having the food in front of her made her stomach growl in earnest. She'd learned a long time ago to never pass up the chance to eat. She took a big bite of her burger. The wash of flavors melted over her tongue. "This is amazing." That was what she tried to say. It came out more like, "Thmpfh mermf mfump."

"Beg pardon?" Cerberus chuckled and chowed on a couple fries, while she chewed and swallowed.

"This is the best burger I've ever had." It wasn't an exaggeration, either.

He shook his head. "It's good, but it's probably not the best."

"How do you know?" She didn't appreciate having her opinion handed to her.

"Because I've been there. Without all the ethereal pollution clogging your senses, they work better."

She didn't believe him, but he believed it. She also didn't care. If this was the diner's hamburger, she wanted *all* the cupcakes. She ate in silence, washing several more bites down with the best freaking cola in history.

When the edge was gone from her hunger, she slowed down and grabbed at her next question. "Give me a straight answer this time. Was my mother happy in the underworld? When Dad says she was terrified of dogs, I assume you've got something to do with that, but… I can't see it." Maybe she wasn't content to let his lies go unnoticed after all.

Cerberus sighed. "Once upon a time, she loved Hades. I don't doubt that. The way they looked at each other? It was the kind of adoration that can't be faked. I know because I saw it fade with time. Eventually I became her captor, at his bidding."

"But she was happy once?"

"And apparently a second time, with your stepfather." His smile was sad. "I'm glad she got that."

A wave of emotion swept through her, stealing Lexi's breath. She didn't know if she was emotionally prepared to dive much further down that hole right now. "Why are we here? Who are we meeting?"

"His name is Paul. He's going to set you up with a new identity and access to funds that can't be traced."

"No." Being in the system, even under an assumed name, meant she could be found.

"You need to be able to move more freely than you do now," Cerberus said.

She shook her head. "Until last night, I was fine with my ability to move about undetected. Besides, once we do what you said"—she wasn't comfortable saying, *free Hades, so he can destroy his brothers*, aloud even in this place—"this all stops, doesn't it?"

"Did The Empire fall when Luke and the rebels blew up the Death Star?"

She didn't want to smile, but it was a subtle reminder of why she liked talking to Cerberus when gods weren't the subject. Dad had been a self-proclaimed OG—Original Geek—and entrenched Lexi in his likes. Cerberus had similar tastes. "I understand what you're saying. There will still be gods out there. I guess I hoped…" What?

"The running would stop?"

That. "Yes."

"It will." His voice was kind. "But it may not be right away, and we have to wait a little longer before we head in. This will serve you in the meantime."

"All right. You realize how much trust I'm putting in you, don't you?" Not as much as she wanted him to believe, but more than she'd given anyone in a long time. She needed to get her information from someone, and so far, everything he'd given her that she could verify checked out. If he thought she was following him blindly, he was more likely to drop his guard.

An empty hole in her chest hoped he was telling her as much of the truth as he was allowed, because she needed someone to lean on.

"How do you know this guy?" she asked.

"Turns out not everyone is faithful to the gods." Cerberus winked.

"You think?"

He laughed. "I knew you'd be surprised. Paul grew up in a religious family. Directly loyal to Thoth, which meant he had access to the education that would teach him the tech. He went through school and hit the real world, and started to question his faith. I found him in a similar forum to the one I located you."

She was familiar with Thoth. When The Enlightenment happened, the gods decided they'd been gone from this world too long, to integrate without help. Most of them weren't interested in learning the technology, but destroying it wasn't an option. People were too addicted to their devices.

So Thoth—with his wisdom and knack for invention—was in charge of collecting a network of loyal humans before the gods made their big debut. People who helped them reach out through modern media and touch most corners of the world. That wasn't how the books taught it. It was phrased more like, *only the most righteous could serve our benevolent lords upon their return*, but Dad taught her to read between the lines.

Cerberus was watching her.

"Are you all right?" she asked.

"Enjoying the view."

The off-the-cuff compliment warmed her, and she fumbled for a response.

"And wondering what kind of obscurity I can toss in your direction, to draw you out a little more—get to know the Lexi raised here, now that I have you face to face. I'm leaning toward an RPG reference. Those are some of my favorites."

The playful teasing was both nice and bittersweet. His observation tugged at an avalanche of memories. She wanted to leave them buried, but as one tumbled loose, they all rolled into her thoughts, which made them tough to grasp. She plucked out one of her favorite. "Instead of bedtime stories, Dad used to read to me from The Monster Compendium. Original edition."

"Most of that was woefully inaccurate."

As she'd discovered when she set out on her own. "It wasn't only about the beholders and drow. He used to tell me…" The words lodged in her throat, stuck on the wave of emotion that came with them.

"It's okay." Cerberus reached across the table and covered her hand. "You don't have to delve into that."

She swallowed. This memory didn't usually hit her so hard. The stress of the last twenty-four hours must be weighing on her. "It's not a big deal. He used to tell me that, if we couldn't destroy the monsters in real life, at least we could roll to do so on paper."

"He sounds like a smart man." The way Cerberus traced his thumb over the back of her hand was comforting.

"He was a genius." She believed so as a ten-year-old, and saw no reason to change that opinion now.

They finished their meal, interspersing bites with more idle chatter. After, Lexi worked her way through two incredible cupcakes, before making herself stop and getting half a dozen more to go.

"They won't taste the same anyplace else," Cerberus said in warning.

Not quite as good was still better than she was used to. "I'll take my chances."

They left the diner, her purchase hanging from her arm in a plastic bag. The mid-morning sun was warm on her face and bare arms. It felt good.

They made small talk as they walked in the direction Cerberus pointed them. It took them into a middle-class suburb. Some of the lawns were manicured, others not so much, and the houses were a lot of the same.

He stopped, a frown marring his features as he sniffed the air. "Something's wrong."

It felt fine to her, but his stance and tone made her forget the heat of the sun. She double tapped her earring, but her view didn't change.

"Wait here," he said and headed up the walk of a nearby home.

She sprinted to catch up. "Like hell, I will."

He shook his head, but didn't pause until he reached the ajar door. "Stay outside."

"Is it dangerous in there?" If it was, she should feel it. But she didn't feel the harpy earlier. Didn't know she was there until she saw it.

"No. But you're not going to like what you see."

She could handle a lot of things. "How do you know?"

"I smell blood. None of it's fresh, but there's a lot."

She hesitated when he pushed open the door, but curiosity won out, and she followed him inside.

The living room was a manifestation of carnage. A man—Paul?—was split from gut to throat, and his entrails and blood spelled out something on the floor.

She couldn't stomach the sight long enough to decipher the Greek. She bolted from the house, barely reaching the edge of the lawn before her lunch surged into her throat, and she emptied the contents of her gut on the grass.

After several retches and a few gasps, she managed to catch her breath. The vulgar images lingered in her head, threatening her with another round of sickness.

A hand rested on her back, and Cerberus rubbed gently. "I don't want to be callous, but we need to go."

Yes. Anywhere but here. She didn't protest, when he tugged her through another siren gateway.

"Why did that happen to him?" she asked as they stepped into a new city. It was the only coherent thought she could grasp.

"It's hard to say for sure."

She didn't care for the vague answer. "Try."

"A harpy found him."

She swallowed past the taste of bile. She needed water. Where was the closest convenience store? Or drinking fountain? Why was she still carrying these stupid cupcakes? "Was this because of me?"

"He's been working with me for years. I assume the message, *For secrets kept,* was meant for me."

His voice was flat, but there was a wilting hint of regret in the words.

The response didn't reassure her. Guilt pounded in her skull, mingling with resentment toward whatever turned her life on its head so suddenly. She was used to looking over her shoulder, but she hated this new and terrifying variant. Loathed it with every fiber of her being.

Allowing herself to feel anything else would lead to her curling up in a ball and sobbing until she couldn't think.

And that kind of surrender would destroy her before the harpy or anything else out there had the chance.

CHAPTER SIX

"I'm done sitting here, doing nothing," Actaeon said.

Even as the words passed his lips, he mentally screamed at himself to take them back. Unlike the visit from Morpheus, part of him knew this was a dream the instant it began. Or rather, it was a memory from forty years ago, that haunted his sleep regularly.

Cassandra rolled to lie on top of him. Her bare skin was soft and smooth against his. He could push her off, but why would he?

"What can I do, to make you stay?" She glided her fingers up his side and shifted to straddle his waist. Her heat teased his hard length. Her tan complexion was dotted by the occasional freckle, culminating in the patches on her cheeks. Her black hair hung down almost to her waist.

"Forever? Nothing. For tonight, keep going." Actaeon pressed up into her, not penetrating, but considering it.

"No." She climbed off and knelt next to him. "I'm done. You're being a stubborn jackass, and I don't know why you won't listen to me."

Because he couldn't. It didn't matter how many times she said she'd seen this play out badly in her visions. The gods were wreaking havoc, forcing faith when it should be freely given and bending the will of the people for their own selfish needs.

"You do know why." Because the last time the gods were in power, three millennia ago, they pitted men against each other in twisted games. Actaeon couldn't watch that happen again.

She climbed from the bed, and he grabbed her wrist. "Cass, please. Don't blame me for this."

She wrenched away and whirled to face him, dark eyes narrowed and flashing with irritation. "Of course I'm blaming you. You're the catalyst. Stay. Home."

"I can't. You know I can't."

She sighed and sank into the chair across from the bed. "Then I'll go with you."

"All right. I'd rather have you by my side, anyway."

Her smile didn't reach her eyes and faded quickly to a grimace. "Me too."

"Come back to bed. Please." He patted the mattress.

She knelt next to him and brushed her lips over his, before standing again. "Not tonight."

From there, the dream tended to skip forward several days, to Actaeon, knocking on Zeus' door. He'd taken up residency in The Reichstag in Germany. Said it suited him. Actaeon pleaded with him to see reason. Told him about the destruction Cassandra had seen at Zeus' hand.

Zeus' response was to send Heracles to kill Cassandra.

Actaeon was grateful his mind glossed over finding her body. Broken. Twisted.

After that, he hunted his cousin down. Found him in Las Vegas. Tried to destroy him. The images of buildings crumbling, people screaming, and streets burning, always filled his head like a rage-filled series of stills. That was all they were back then, though. Anger had consumed him. All he wanted was vengeance for her.

The problem was he and Heracles were equally matched. He was a better sniper, Heracles was a stronger fighter, and they did enough damage to each other that they wound up unconscious at the end of the fight.

Actaeon had woken up to a city in ruins. So many people dead, caught in the crossfire.

He pried his eyes open and sat up in bed. He'd lived that night in 2028 a million times in his dreams, and the outcome never changed. Was that how it was for Cassandra before it happened?

He'd tried to find her after she died. Journeyed to the underworld. Paid the toll and faced numerous trials. She wasn't there. If she hadn't made it back then, there was no reason to think she'd be there today. Her vague vision must have led her to interpret something wrong.

He shook off the dream as best he could, so not at all. The clock next to his bed said it was barely midnight. He needed a drink.

He strolled the few blocks to a bar that dealt in metal currency, found a table in the back corner, and paid for a bottle of tequila. He downed the first shot and moved on to his second. The images lingered in his mind, but they were more of a blur now.

Actaeon was starting on his third, when a familiar scent reached his nostrils. Three-headed lapdog. He pushed his chair from the table as Cerberus sat down across from him.

"Stay?" Cerberus said.

"That's my line."

Cerberus growled. "I'll buy your next drink."

"I'm set, thanks." Actaeon held up the bottle.

It wasn't that he had an issue with Cerberus, personally. Actaeon didn't care for any servant. They were required to swear loyalty to a god—not necessarily the one who created them—in order to survive. He didn't begrudge them that, but it meant none of them could be trusted.

Cerberus could be the most loyal creature in the world. To Persephone. To Lexi. But if Hades ordered him to do something contrary to what Cerberus had promised another being, Cerberus didn't have a choice.

"Do you want me to have them bring you a bowl?" Actaeon asked. "Make you more comfortable?"

"That's never been funny."

True, but it had always irritated the fuck out of the hellhound, which made it worthwhile. Actaeon sat again, though he wasn't sure why, and waved the bartender over, to ask for a second shot glass. "Where's your ward?"

"Close enough I can smell her. Far enough your aura won't wake her up." Cerberus settled in his seat.

Actaeon sniffed the air. Indeed, that familiar, tempting scent hid underneath the stench of liquor, cigarettes, and hellhound. He must be off his game, if he hadn't noticed her sooner. He didn't need to ask how Cerberus found him. The dog was traveling via siren gate, the same as Actaeon had, and those only went so many places at the same time. The power cycles ran differently through various parts of the world.

Even if Cerberus wasn't looking for him, odds were decent they'd end up in the same city if they were traveling at the same time and both wanted to stay in the US.

Actaeon should have gone to Australia. "What can I do for you?"

"Come with us."

One-trick puppy, this guy was. "You're not my type. I'd come with her, though."

Cerberus growled.

Correction. Two-trick puppy. Actaeon stood again. "Catch you around. Or hopefully not."

"It's a chance for vengeance. For Cassandra." Cerberus' words hit Actaeon's back with a hard slap.

"Last time I tried to do that, it cost too many lives. Not doing it again."

"You didn't have Hades on your side last time."

Actaeon whirled to face him. He leaned over, rested his hands on the back of the chair, and locked his gaze on the hellhound's face. "No one can kill Heracles."

"Anyone can be killed." Cerberus didn't flinch. "And with Hades here, the balance of power shifts—"

"If it means swearing fealty to another dickhead with a faith fetish, I'm out. Sorry, puppy. Not all of us were made to serve." He spoke through clenched teeth, irritation and ambivalence raging inside. The old him would have said *yes*. But he knew better now. There was a price to pay, and he wasn't willing to fund it with random casualties.

"We're going, either way. As soon as the veil is thin enough to take Lexi through. She can't be out in the open any longer."

Actaeon didn't want to care. He shouldn't still be here. "You can't take her into the labyrinth."

"It's her choice. Save her by being there with us."

"One life, in exchange for hundreds? Thousands? Nope. Have fun." He turned and walked out of the bar, stuffing his doubt and self-loathing back into the box that sat at the bottom of his gut.

He returned to his hotel room, but sleep was a long way off. He settled into the easy chair by the bed and turned on the TV. His options were infomercials, syndicated TV shows, or evangelical diatribes for the local deity.

A fire-and-brimstone preacher bestowed the virtues of Ares on the masses. *War. Wonderful.* TV hadn't changed in nearly a century.

Actaeon tried to tune out the preacher, but that meant falling into his memories of that last night with Cassandra. And when he was awake, he remembered it all.

"That's not an answer anymore." Actaeon *hated arguing with Cassandra, but he was getting tired of* because I said so *as an explanation.*

She glided her fingers down the front of her blouse, undoing buttons as she went, until the shirt hung open, hinting at what was underneath. "Wouldn't you rather play, than talk politics?"

"No. What did you see? Why is it so incredibly important we step aside and let the gods have their way, when that goes against everything we believe?"

She sat on the couch with a sigh. As a general rule, he understood her reluctance to share what she'd seen. Being burdened with the ability to glimpse the possible future was hard on her, and telling someone else details frequently created a self-fulfilling prophecy of sorts.

This time he couldn't wrap his head around it. She insisted standing up to the gods in their recent bid to force humanity to worship them would cost more than it would prevent. Actaeon didn't want to destroy lives, but people were dying anyway. "Isn't there anything you can do, to give me a hint?" He softened his voice.

"You'll lose me. Possibly more than once."

Her statement knotted in his gut. "How?"

She shook her head. "No details."

He didn't want that. They were good together. But ignoring the situation was the equivalent of burying his head in the sand. "Are you going to leave me, for being stubborn?" His attempt at a joke came out strained.

"This fight will kill me. It will destroy you, but you'll still survive."

"No. No. No." He didn't want to hear it after all. If she'd seen it, it would happen regardless. She was delaying the inevitable by asking him to not act. Or she was making sure it happened. Fuck. This was why he wasn't supposed to ask. He had to do what he would, either way. He knelt in front of her and took her hands in his. "Destruction of your soul, or simple death?"

Her smile was sad. "I'll go to the underworld. I won't be gone forever. And you'll find a way to get to me, though it will take a while."

A while could be anywhere from a week to three centuries—or beyond. "Then we'll be back together again."

"I don't know."

His frown deepened. "You can't stop the story there. I need an answer."

"That's the answer. The real answer. I don't know. I can't see past our being reunited in the underworld. Something hides the rest."

"Because you'll cease to exist?"

"Maybe. I've never seen my soul destroyed before, so possibly, but I don't think that's it. What comes after is hidden. Like it's behind a locked door."

He let the words sink in, while he stroked the back of her hand and studied her eyes. There were no answers there. "You know I'm going to do this regardless." He hated having the knowledge that his actions would separate them and being compelled to follow through anyway. Dating an oracle meant not letting indecision paralyze him, though. Fate was a bitch like that. If it was set, it was set.

"If you do, then promise me something."

"Anything," he said.

"Once I'm gone, sometime down the line, you'll meet someone else like me."

"Who can see the future?"

"I don't know." She shrugged. "I have an impression, no details. She's hidden. But not like my fate. Like an illusion. But do whatever she needs. Help her. And you'll see me again."

Actaeon dragged himself from a memory that had never been more than torture to relive before tonight. Cassandra couldn't have been talking about Lexi. Who wasn't going to the underworld anyway. Lexi was walking into the labyrinth.

Besides, Cassandra was his past, and the only way to learn from it was to not go making the same mistakes again.

CHAPTER SEVEN

When Cerberus returned to the hotel room he got them for the night, Lexi was sitting on her bed, knees pulled to her chest. She glared at him. Red rimmed her eyes and splotched her cheeks.

"Are you all right?" Concern spilled through him. After they left Paul's, she was a wreck of jumbled nerves and thoughts. Not that Cerberus blamed her.

But after talking and the best over-the-counter sleep aids money could buy, she'd fallen asleep. He wouldn't have left her alone if Hades didn't demand he seek out Actaeon.

She shook her head. "I'm exhausted. Now I have those damn pills inside me, and I can't stop seeing it. All the blood and…" She shuddered and hugged herself.

Cerberus settled onto the mattress facing her, close enough his knees touched her feet.

There were windows when he could take her through the veil. He'd planned to spend the next a few weeks showing her how to focus, meditate, and access her gifts more naturally.

After what they saw today, he didn't think they had that long. Focus was necessary, at the very least. Now was as good a time as any, to show her how to clear her mind in a stressful situation. "How did Persephone meet your stepdad?" he asked.

She stared at him, expression blank. "What?"

"Is it a happy story?"

Lexi nodded.

"Tell me about it. And keep it at the front of your mind, when you need something positive to grasp."

"Where should I start?"

He smiled to reassure her. "Wherever you'd like."

"I don't think this will help." Agony filled her voice. "Will we be here much longer? What if they find us again? What if they find another person they think is working with us? What if—"

He rested a hand on her arm, drawing her gaze. "It will help. But this should too—the labyrinth is in a place between places, and we have to wait until the veil is thin to take you through. We'll be able to go in two days." He glanced at the clock. "I guess technically, it'll be tomorrow. Two more sleeps."

"Prepare me? For what? I know how to mask myself behind illusion and hide. I'm not some supersecret, magic kung-fu chick, suppressing my mad kickboxing skills."

"You don't need to be. I'm not tossing you in a fighting arena." He kept his tone soothing. "The prep we're doing is up here." He trailed a finger along the side of her face, toward her ear, to point at her head.

She gave a strained laugh. "I'm already mental."

"This is to help you focus on the gift you have. Your power. And it will also help you cope with grief, horror—anything that threatens to overwhelm you."

"What's it like? This place we're going?"

He frowned as he tried to think of the best way help her understand it. "It's ethereal. As in, it's not a physical place. So you'll leave your body behind."

"Leave it where?"

This wasn't what he had in mind to distract her, but she needed to know, and if it drew her out of her shell, he'd take it. "It's hard to describe. Kind of in limbo? It's safe, though. It's like a single-unit stasis field, if that makes it easier to picture."

"It does." She relaxed her arms and uncurled, matching his cross-legged posture. "What does the labyrinth look like?"

"I can only tell you what I've seen, but it won't matter. It changes depending on who enters. But for you, the illusions won't be there. You'll see it for what it really is. That's why it's so important you be there with me." That was the theory, anyway. He wanted to tell her the truth—that he didn't know for sure if it would work that way—but Hades forbade it. Explicitly. *Don't tell her you don't know for sure.*

"And if I see through the illusion, we can walk right through it? Straight to the underworld, or Hades?" She sounded skeptical.

No. Definitely not. There would still be monsters to fight. Other trials to confront. He wasn't allowed to tell her most of that, either. "There will be other things, but it's my job to handle those."

"If it's that easy, why hasn't anyone done it before now?"

"Because it's not that easy."

"Careful," Hades said in his head.

Cerberus gathered his thoughts, to make sure he didn't give the wrong thing away. Not that he'd be able to, but it would look odd if he tried to say the words, and Hades' commands kept him from speaking. "You're the only one of you there is. To everyone else, the illusions are real."

"Oh." She fiddled with a loose thread on the blanket beneath her, mouth twisted.

He couldn't tell if it was disbelief or mistrust marring her features. "Tell me about how your parents met," he prompted again.

She searched his face, then shook her head. "When Dad was in his early twenties, he and his friends would have gaming weekends. Basically, as soon as work was over, Friday night, they'd all get together at someone's house and role play. Frequently, around two or three Sunday morning, they'd realize they'd been up since Friday before work. And they'd go out to eat at the diner where Mom worked."

"So after the first couple of times, no one was really surprised?" This was good. Moving away from sensitive topics. He didn't like feeling as though she could see through his lies. Her gift was to see physical truths, not unspoken ones, but guilt still clawed inside at what he kept from her. He hoped she'd forgive him if the reality came out.

Lexi didn't like the sensation that Cerberus was lying to her. There wasn't a strong voice inside insisting what he said was untrue, but it was too simple. If the only thing needed to get to Hades was seeing through illusions, Lorelei could have rigged something for someone, or there had to be other ways.

She didn't call him on it, because she was curious to see how long he'd keep up the deception. She was worried about what they might really find in the maze, but even though he was keeping secrets, she believed without a doubt that he'd go out of his way to protect her.

She forced her concern from her face and answered his question. "No. I suppose they expected it, after a while. Most likely planned it, since the weekend graveyard waitress was Mom. At first he used the gaming night as an excuse to visit her, but after several months, he'd go in alone when it wasn't a gaming night, and they'd chat. Flirt. Go out when her shift was up."

"Was she happy?"

Lexi nodded. "The way he talks about her, and knowing he was a good guy, I'd say *yes*. He was with her when she went into labor with me. He says he saw us post-delivery, mother and daughter, and knew he couldn't leave us alone." The memory of his adoration as he told the story lodged in her throat. "So he asked her to marry him the day I was born."

What came after, though—the death, the pain… Her head throbbed, and she gasped at the shock of emotion and pain. She clenched her fist around the blanket, squeezing until the wave passed. When she opened her eyes, Cerberus was watching her.

The laugh she gave to brush it off was strangled. "So, what's your story?" She forced the question out.

"I… uh… serve Hades. Do what I'm commanded. Um… I've never had to fetch the paper."

Her laugh came more naturally this time, though pain lingered inside. "And you like classic sci-fi."

"Star Wars isn't science fiction. It's a genre of its own." His serious tone caught her off guard.

"You sound like Dad."

"He sounds like a smart man."

She was able to breathe again, and relished the long, steady breaths. "He was. How did you become a fan?"

"After Hades was imprisoned, I spent a lot of time here. More than I ever had before. I was looking for Persephone. For you. I've had forty years of intermittent free time to catch up with the world."

"So there's more to you than servitude," she said in a teasing tone.

He shook his head. "You're supposed to be figuring out meditation. Learning to find your center. Not grilling me."

"Fine." She huffed, but she didn't mind. She wasn't sure if he did it on purpose or not, but the conversation helped keep her calm. Better than drifting into so many dark places, including those currently hidden from her in her skull.

Lexi was surprised to see she'd slept until after noon. She drifted off last night at the end of a meditation session that worked wonders for her temporary psyche. The dream she had helped her feel better too.

It wasn't the first time Mom visited her in her sleep, but it had been a few weeks. Last night, she was as warm and friendly as ever, asking when Lexi would be there and introducing her to a new friend.

Cerberus looked up from the TV when she sat in bed.

"Did you sleep?" she asked.

He shook his head. "I'm keeping an eye on you."

He hadn't done that last night, when he wandered away without warning, after drugging her. Sure, she'd requested the pills, but still… She had a feeling he wouldn't give her a straight answer about where he'd gone, even if she did point it out. "You have to sleep sometime, right? Have you been awake since you found me?"

"I don't actually *need* to. It's like you and sweets. It's a pleasant treat, but it doesn't impact my survival."

She quirked her mouth in disbelief. "I hate to argue—"

His snort cut her off.

She smiled at the good-natured jab. "Okay, I don't. But sweets are most certainly necessary. Life deprives us of enough, without us intentionally passing up cake."

"You know what I mean. But I promise I never pass up on a nap when it's an option."

"Good." She climbed from the bed. "Speaking of, I'm having cupcakes for breakfast." She grabbed the box from its perch near the TV, picked one out, and bit into it. The flavor that washed over her tongue was sweet, but not what she'd experienced yesterday.

"I tried to warn you," Cerberus said. "The aura pollution changes the way everything tastes."

The horror of yesterday and the looming fear, gnawed at the back of her mind. But the meditation last night helped her box it away. To haunt her nightmares later, she was sure. With a little luck, not until after this was over.

She ate the cupcakes, despite the fact that they were no longer the best she'd ever tasted. It was cake for breakfast, and she was going to enjoy it.

Cerberus drained the last of his coffee. "We'll go in the morning. Do you want to get in a couple more hours of practice first?"

"I don't get how meditating is going to help me in a hostile situation. I won't be able to sit down and focus."

"If you recognize your power, it will make you even more effective when it comes to distinguishing other people's."

She wasn't convinced. "My *power*? As in my aura? I already recognize it. It's purple and pink."

"That's a visual representation. You already do this to an extent. In New York, you could tell Poseidon from Prometheus. This is a matter of discerning in more detail, and then being able to do it on command instead of having to concentrate first."

That actually sounded pretty useful. "What do I have to do?"

"Close your eyes and look inside. Start by finding the threads you know belong to you."

She did as he instructed, watching as she listened.

"Now separate out those that are mine," he said.

She gave a slight nod but was more intent on executing his lesson.

"From there, sift through and start picking out other distinct strands."

"Just like that?" she asked.

"Well, no. But I don't know another way to describe it."

She would have rolled her eyes if they weren't closed, but she concentrated on following the vague teaching anyway. At first, it seemed useless. It was all static outside of the room.

But the longer she searched, the more she picked wisps out of the background noise. Whispers of other people. She couldn't tell if they had weak auras or were far away. It was a neat trick, regardless.

She traipsed along the signatures of energy, following one thread to the next.

Actaeon. The name slid into her thoughts before she registered that was whom she felt.

She opened her eyes and directed her gaze at Cerberus. "He's in this city. Why didn't you say something?"

"There are a lot of people in this city." He turned his attention to his hands, but he never asked *who*.

"Are we here because he is?"

"We're here because this was what was available."

Lexi pursed her lips. "Why are we in the same city as Actaeon, and why didn't you tell me?" Did it matter? According to her dream, it did. According to her sense of self-preservation, too, but for the opposite reason.

"I was hoping he'd go with us," Cerberus said.

"I've talked to the guy twice, and I could have told you his answer would be *no*." Realization spread through her. "Why do you need someone like him on this trip?" Someone who could summon a bow from nothing? Who could kill a gargoyle with a single arrow? "Wait. Don't tell me. It's because this isn't as easy as you're making it sound."

Cerberus worked his jaw up and down, but no sound came out.

She shouldn't be surprised—she figured that was the case—but having the suspicions confirmed devoured her. "In the twenty-ish years since Dad's death, I've stayed safe. Sure, I've had a couple close calls, but nothing that terrified me and made me wonder if my guts were going to be on the floor in a couple of hours. In the last two days, since meeting you in person, that's changed."

"You can't blame me for a series of coincidences."

"I can, and I do, because you keep leaving gaps in your explanations." She tugged on her shoes, grabbed her backpack, and headed for the door. "I'm done."

CHAPTER EIGHT

Now that Lexi had sensed Actaeon, she couldn't ignore him. He was like a familiar flavor that lingered on the tongue even after the source faded. She headed in the opposite direction. Not that a few more blocks would make it easier to ignore him.

She walked, not having a destination in mind. It was tempting to hop a bus and ride out of the city. She was going back at the end of the night, though. This was to make Cerberus sweat. Prove she still had some say in her own life.

But she'd go with him. It didn't matter how dangerous it may be or if anybody else went with them. This trip meant seeing Mom; an opportunity to actually meet Persephone in person. Cerberus didn't get to know that. If he was keeping secrets from her, she had the right to do the same.

Lexi walked until her feet ached and the sun was vanishing behind the horizon, then headed into the nearest bar. She knew better than to lose herself in alcohol, but two beers in, she was enjoying a faint buzz and considering if she should eat before she started on the third bottle.

That distinct flavor of ice drew closer. She didn't know what it was about Actaeon—why, out of all the encounters she'd had in her life, she was drawn to him. If she squinted, in her chemically-induced chill, she swore she saw a faint cord stretch from her to the door.

Which he just walked through. And there was definitely no thread attaching them.

He didn't glance at her, and she turned her attention back to her drink. Maybe she should order a burger or something.

The ice moved closer, embracing her. She didn't like how soothing it was. Didn't care for the threat of dropping her guard.

He set a drink in front of her, then took the seat across from her. "Bartender assures me this is what you're having."

Lexi looked at the chocolate martini, then at her local microbrew, before landing her gaze on him. "And you believed him?"

"Why would he lie?"

The question drew a sarcastic snort that tugged loose her frustration with Cerberus. "Why does anyone lie? Maybe they do it for preservation— theirs or someone else's. Or perhaps it's for shits, grins, and giggles. Oh, I know—because they can."

"Or because their master orders them to. I've been there." He leaned back in his chair and stretched out his legs.

She tried not to let her gaze wander over the way his casual pose emphasized the definition of muscle under his clothes. Struggled to ignore the strength and passion he worked so hard to bottle up. She mentally shook her head, to clear away the thought. "Why did you really buy me the drink?" She took a sip. It wasn't bad. Better than the cupcakes.

Which, now that she thought about it, were the only thing she'd eaten since yesterday. She downed the rest of the martini.

"Instinct told me to," he said.

"Do you listen to instinct a lot?"

Sarcasm tinged his smile. "As infrequently as possible. But sometimes fate wins out, despite our best efforts. What did Cerberus lie to you about?"

"What makes you think he did?"

"You've been with a servant for a few days now. He's lied about something. Everyone who deals with gods does."

"What will you lie to me about?" She didn't ask the question with malice. In fact, it struck her as odd but pleasant how easily the conversation flowed.

Actaeon leaned in, grabbed her beer, and took a drag off it. "Caring. What did he lie about?"

Did that mean he did care or he didn't?

She didn't want to think about it. "The lies all kind of runs together until it's hard to pick one from the next. He didn't tell me you were in the same town as us."

"You didn't want to see me?" The fake hurt in his voice was undercut with something more seductive.

"You haven't gone out of your way to avoid me?"

He shook his head. "Maybe. Not tonight."

"Why on other nights?" She liked watching him move. Each move of his frame was like a calculated adjustment. He reminded her of a hunter, stalking his prey. Did that make her the prey? In any other context, that would push her away, but with him it sent possibility racing over her skin.

"If you weren't the daughter of a god, when you climbed into my cab I would have asked if you wanted to take a detour."

Detour. A simple word that sent images racing through her thoughts, carried on the reminder of the brief touches they'd shared. What would it feel like, to have his hands roaming her body? "Do you do that a lot?"

"When I want to get laid." It was blunt. Direct. Honest.

She couldn't have asked for a more perfect combination. "How often does it work?" She leaned in and rested her forearms on the table. Her T-shirt wouldn't show off much cleavage, but it was still a good look for her.

He smirked. "Often enough that I've been doing it for decades. Sometimes I get turned down, others I don't. But you recognized me. You reek of the gods. And that's dangerous. There's one thing I always keep in mind when it comes to our *benevolent* overlords."

"The gods and their servants can't be trusted?"

"Sexy *and* smart. Lethal combination."

She bit her bottom lip. This was the oddest flirting she'd ever been party to, but she didn't think for a moment it was anything but. "What if hooking up with me wasn't taking a side?" Why did she use that terminology? *Instinct.* The word sounded in her head in his voice.

"It would be."

"Not by me." She looked around. "And there's no one else here."

His smile grew into something hungry. "Hmm… Do you want to take a detour from your night?"

The words circled her thoughts on tantalizing ice, wrapping her up in need. She didn't care if it was a fling. This man, apathy wrapped in ambivalence, spoke to something at her core. "Yes."

He grasped her fingers as he stood, and a shock raced through her. It was similar to the sensation in Hawaii, but more. She looked at their hands and the way fuchsia wove with ice. She'd never seen auras do that. Then again, she hadn't spent a lot of time with anyone else who had one.

She didn't bother to ask about condoms. Her godly parentage meant no chance of contracting STD's, and reproduction didn't work the same way for immortals.

He led her toward the restroom sign at the back of the bar, nudged her into the single room, and locked the door behind them. There was a sink and a toilet, and not much else, but it was clean aside from the gray of age.

"I don't know what to make of you, the woman who shouldn't exist. But since you do…" Actaeon pressed his chest into her back and glided his hands up her stomach, over her shirt.

Desire crackled across her skin and tightened in her nipples.

He pointed her toward the mirror.

There were no auras in their reflection. Lexi only saw them. Did he give her this view on purpose? "Since I do?"

"There's nothing more to the thought." He tugged her hair, to expose her neck. The way he kissed along her skin was desperate, tingling through her like a scratch on an itch she didn't know she had.

She didn't know if her reaction was all physical, or if there were traces of ethereal in there. She'd think about it later. It had been too long since she got laid, and even longer since she felt like she could lose herself in it. With his touch, intense and demanding, gliding over her, she could do exactly that.

When he bit her shoulder, her need spiked, centered in her belly and unfurling through her veins. She groaned and pressed back into him. Everything about him was hard and solid. The skin-on-skin contact was heat encased in ice.

He met her gaze in the mirror, and she was struck by the contrast. The visual that insisted they were normal people screwing in a bathroom bar, and the ethereal sensations that proved otherwise.

"I'm not in the mood for foreplay." His voice was gruff.

She couldn't agree more. Dampness pooled between her legs. She fumbled with her jeans, undoing them half a second before he shoved them down her legs, scraping flesh and leaving a delicious burn behind.

He followed the curve of her ass with his hand, gliding between her thighs.

His touch slipped along her skin. "So fucking wet." When he spoke, the words vibrated in her soul. She didn't think that was an exaggeration.

Actaeon nudged her opening with the head of his cock, dipping in enough to stretch her out, before pulling back again.

"You said no foreplay." Need lined her voice.

He smirked. "But a little teasing is good for everyone."

He slid inside her without further warning, gripping her hip with one hand. The sudden penetration filled her up and drew a gasp of surprise. He felt incredible.

The playfulness gave way to frantic pounding. She dug her fingers into the edge of the sink for something to grip. She almost swore the porcelain cracked under her grip.

Each time he slammed against her, he struck the right chord, drawing her to the edge of climax.

He met her gaze in the mirror again, and heat sparked in his normally icy eyes. He moved his free hand to seek out the spot between her legs begging for attention.

When he brushed her clit, she almost came, but he edged off before she hit that peak.

She sank into the pleasure of the fast and frantic. It wasn't just the penetration or the sex. The current of aura and power flowed between them. They were intangible, but she still felt it.

Climax inched up and overtook her without warning, crashing around her in a wash that sparked in her veins and pulsed behind her eyelids.

She felt him when he came, energy spilling inside her, mingling with hers, and drawing out her own orgasm. Her thoughts were gone. Vanished in a cloud of sensation she couldn't describe beyond, *Dear goddess Aphrodite that was fucking incredible.*

She suspected Actaeon wouldn't appreciate the exclamation. She was grateful to let the heavy breathing in the small room be the only exchange. For a heartbeat, he looked different. Younger? No.

But his expression hardened. Like that, whatever she saw was gone.

Maybe she'd imagined it. Endorphins or shitty lighting or something.

He touched the fresh piercing in her ear—the cuff from Lorelei. "Don't rely on this." His breath was hot on her skin.

"Why not?"

"How much do you want to know?"

She had a choice? "Everything."

"No, you don't." His reflection was a twisted mask of melancholy and determination.

She wasn't putting up with this again. "You don't get to decide that any more than anyone else."

"I'll tell you what I'm able to." It wasn't a promise of *everything*, but it was closer to saying he'd give her the truth than she'd gotten from anyone else.

"Thank you."

Actaeon ordered them two burgers when they returned to their table. He paused and looked at Lexi. "Unless you're a vegetarian?"

She shook her head, a soft smile tugging up her lips. "Where's yours?" she asked.

She was talking about his siren piece. He trailed his thumb under his collar, hooked it under the familiar leather cord, and pulled the onyx pendant free to show her. It was a basic, smooth stone. To the naked eye, it was a simple necklace.

"You rely on yours," she said.

"It's not the same. Mine keeps master and servant from finding me, but it isn't a link to my sanity."

She frowned.

"Your puppy has one too. It's how he creates doors so easily." Actaeon left off a key piece of information here. He didn't want to lie to Lexi, but this was one of those things she couldn't change, because Cerberus had made the decision, and it wouldn't help her any. Cerberus only needed the gate key because of her. He could shed his mortal skin and pass between the physical and ethereal whenever he wanted.

"Can yours do that too?"

"No. Definitely not." He winced at the force behind his denial. "I call Lorelei when I need a gate."

Their food arrived, and she nibbled on a fry. "Why?"

He'd promised to tell her what he could. Might as well put it out there. "The price on what Cerberus has is too steep for me."

"What did it cost?"

The same thing any high-end stone from a siren cost. "A favor."

"That must be worse than it sounds."

"It's exactly what it sounds like. If Cerberus has a siren gate key, it means he owes her something.

He's bound to do that one favor when she calls it in, regardless of what it is. It can be anything, as long as he's capable. It doesn't matter who dies—him… someone else… It's a binding contract."

It might even be stronger than Cerberus' bond with Hades. Not that Actaeon knew of anyone stupid enough to test that theory.

"Oh." Her frown deepened. She took a bite of her food, then shoved her plate aside. "What did yours cost?"

He gave a dry chuckle. Nothing he wasn't willing to pay. He never promised more than he could afford. "She gets to try to break me. The how, like with the favor, is up to her." Over the years, she focused on defining that as *rough sex*. Her pleasure lay in the fact he complied with her requests because he needed something.

He didn't have a problem with that.

Lexi alternated between worrying her lip and working her jaw up and down. "How do you know anything about mine?" she finally asked.

"I used to date an oracle." He meant to toss the response out there as casually as anything else, but the memories were fresher than normal. The affection wasn't there, though.

He'd moved on from Cassandra, but the regret still lingered. The one question he could never afford to ask, but did anyway—*what if I'd done things differently?*

CHAPTER NINE

Lexi didn't know how to process the information. Not that she was surprised Actaeon had a past; that was a given. But Lexi was supposed to be unique.

This was what she got for taking anything Cerberus said at face value. If she were the only one, they wouldn't have a name for it. "Did she see through illusions too?"

"Not quite. Okay, not at all. She saw the future. The truth of what was to come."

That was actually pretty different. There was a rush of relief that Cerberus was telling the truth about that.

"That would suck." Lexi might not like the weird double-vision that came with her birthright, but having her life laid out for her and *knowing* it? No thank you.

His laugh was strained. "It did. For the longest time, she had a cuff like yours that kept her from glimpsing too much. Not that she saw everything to begin with, but when the earring broke, she got caught in the wash of what she'd missed. It was information overload."

That double sucked. Lexi tried to picture how that would work in her case, and couldn't. Probably for the best, if experiencing it was linked to her sanity.

"She recovered, but it haunted her." His expression said it did a bit of the same to him. "She felt it all more distinctly. Spent too much time trying to change what couldn't be changed."

"Wait. No. Nope. Uh-uh. No way." Lexi refused to believe it. "That means the future is set in stone."

"Parts of it are."

She shook her head, but he looked so serious, she didn't think arguing would do her any good. If he was giving her answers, though, she'd ask the one Cerberus held back the most about. "This place where Hades is, the labyrinth—how dangerous is it?"

He studied her for a moment, brow furrowed, as if she'd asked something ludicrous. "It's holding the most powerful god in history prisoner. He's been there for the last fifty years, and he's so desperate to get out, he's willing to sacrifice his own daughter, to find a loophole in the trap."

"Right." Maybe she didn't care for the full-on truth of the situation, after all. The bluntness made her pulse hammer in her ears. "But Cerberus…"

"Would probably do anything to protect you."

She nodded, grateful he not only finished her thought, but also sounded like he agreed.

"Unless he's ordered to do otherwise. He's a servant first. Like he was when he kept Persephone bound to the underworld." Actaeon's expression softened. "I'm not trying to be cruel. This is what you're asking for."

And it made her even more certain going down there was the right thing. She didn't deserve this, but neither did Mom. "It's okay. I appreciate you not sugar-coating it. It's a lot to process, is all."

"I bet. I've had my whole life to process, and it's still tough sometimes."

"How long is that?"

"My life?" He sounded amused. "It's hard to track across different calendars, but I'm about 3700 years old."

And she dreaded the day she was halfway to one-hundred. "Can you show me where this labyrinth is without Cerberus?"

"Nope. Not now, not ever. Did you hear what I said about it? Why would you want to go down there, anyway? To say *hi* to a god you've never met, because he was your sperm donor? You don't owe him anything."

She hesitated. How much did she trust him with? He'd given her information, but that didn't mean it was an altruistic offer. So why did she feel like she could tell him anything? "Dad, the man who raised me despite hating the god I came from, is my family. The only father I have, as far as I'm concerned."

"Then… why would you free Hades?"

"He knows where Mom is." She winced as she said the words. It was too much to give away.

Actaeon's shocked expression agreed. "Persephone is dead. That's one truth I'm so sorry to be blunt about, but it's true."

"I know. But there's the underworld, right? Purgatory? She's in one of those." Great. Now she sounded like a crack-pot. She'd come off even worse when he asked why she thought so.

"That's possible. Sometimes we don't end up there—especially those of us touched by the gods. Life just ends, and our souls cease to exist. At least, that's the assumption."

"She's down there. I've seen it."

Pity passed across his face.

"Don't," she snapped. "It was a dream. More like several of them. Over the past few years. She visits me in my sleep."

He pinched the bridge of his nose. "You're going to make me destroy all of your hopes tonight, aren't you? Morpheus—"

"I know who the god of sleep is." She might not have cared for direct answers, but the harsh truth was better than being condescended to. "This is her. Not some manifestation plucked from my subconscious."

"You can't *know*."

"I get that." Anger was creeping in. Why had she opened up to him? Why were they still talking? She had to make him understand, and she didn't know why. "But I believe it."

"We don't get to have faith. Things are or they aren't. There's no wondering. We do know."

Lexi didn't want to think about how much harder life would be if that was the case. "I don't care what you say. Faith keeps us alive. Maybe not faith in the gods, but that the sun will come up in the morning and that the booze will be good and that not all people are assholes. Faith is a reason for living."

He sighed.

So much for making a convincing case.

"Then I can't change your mind?" he said.

"I was going to ask you the same. Because you're coming with me." She didn't know where her certainty came from. More whispers of her recent dream flitted back, and understanding spread through her.

His eyes grew wide. "What makes you believe that?"

"There was another woman last night, when Mom came to visit me. She had dark hair and skin. She was freckled. And she said you'd go with me."

"No."

Lexi expected that. This was her opportunity to laugh the whole thing off. Tell him it was a joke, and she was impressed he didn't fall for it. She wanted to do that. But she couldn't. "This woman said she was glad I found you. She promised you'd go with me."

"She's dead, and no one speaks for me but me."

"Mom's dead too. Faith, right? Is not knowing they're out there worth the risk?"

Is losing Actaeon? Or your life?

The odd thought jarred her, and she couldn't place it. Something told her this wasn't the kind of guy who died easily. Or at all.

That's not the only way to lose someone.

She looked at him and the indecision that reflected her own. Did she want him to agree or refuse?

Cerberus flexed his fingers and resisted the urge to pace.

Go get her, Hades' command reverberated in his skull long after it was given.

He would. Cerberus would retrieve her soon, in plenty of time to make it through the veil. He was going to give her as long as possible to cool off, before dragging her in.

Not that he wanted to do any dragging at all, but this was one of those orders he wasn't allowed to refuse. She was within reach, and for now, that was enough. In about an hour, it wouldn't be.

When he felt her aura shift and her scent grow stronger, relief spilled inside. She was coming back on her own.

He sniffed the air and frowned. She wasn't alone. Actaeon's presence wasn't just nearby, it was also mingled with hers. Every muscle in Cerberus' body tensed as they grew closer.

Lexi pushed into the hotel room with Actaeon by her side. She looked at Cerberus with a tight smile. "I'm ready, and I brought a friend."

"I see that." Cerberus should feel better. This was what Hades wanted. The faint flush in Lexi's skin and the smell of sex that clung to her made defensiveness surge inside. And possibly a thread of jealousy. He squelched the latter and looked at Actaeon. "What changed your mind?"

Actaeon smirked. "A persuasive woman."

Lexi rolled her eyes, but her smile relaxed. "How does this work? Do you open one of those doorways somewhere, and we simply walk into this labyrinth?"

"Pretty much." There was more to the magic and mechanics of it, but that was a fair enough summary.

"This will stay with your body, though." Actaeon trailed his finger along the edge of her ear, over the siren piercing.

The gesture was blatantly intimate, especially given the slight tilt of her head into his touch. "So, no bodies… What will we look like?" she asked.

"In theory, we'll look the way we see ourselves. Probably not a whole lot different than now." Cerberus forced himself not to speak through clenched teeth. What and whom she did in her free time was none of his business. "It all feels tangible."

"In theory?" Concern filled Lexi's question.

"That's how it works for me," Cerberus said. "But I've never taken an oracle down there before."

Lexi dragged in a breath. "Right. Let's get this over with."

"And you're sure you're going with us?" Cerberus asked Actaeon.

"To Hell and back."

It wasn't funny, but Cerberus chuckled. It was better than thinking about how every single part of this, from the setup to the participants to the steps in-between, felt like a massive mistake.

Lexi didn't know how Cerberus knew or why it was any of his business, but the glare he kept focused on Actaeon was disquieting and unjustified.

It lasted while they headed toward their destination, and as Cerberus gave her the run-down one more time and asked if she had any last-minute questions. He only paused when he squeezed her hand. "Step through the wall. Just like Platform Nine and Three-Quarters. I'll see you on the other side."

"All right." She had no idea what that meant, but it didn't seem relevant. She tried to sound confident, despite the fear roaring inside. Mom promised this would be all right. That Lexi would find her. That Actaeon and Cerberus would keep her safe.

It would be all right.

Or she'd walk into that brick wall, faceplant, and fall back on her ass. Everyone would have a good laugh, and they'd turn around and go back to their regularly scheduled lives.

She braced herself, squeezed Cerberus's hand tight, and walked through the wall.

There was nothing. The noise of the city vanished. The ever-present weight of other people's auras—her own—the stench of car exhaust, the sensation of anything on her skin—it was all gone. There was also no screech of siren music or pounding headache, like the other gates she'd stepped through.

"That wasn't so bad." She kept the joking in her voice as she turned to Cerberus and Actaeon.

They weren't there. Her heart sank.

She spun around. Everything was hazy. Not black or white. Just gray, as far as the eye could see.

Panic nudged her senses, and she stepped forward. There wasn't any ground beneath her feet. She looked down and vertigo swept through her. Nothing stopped her from moving in any direction. "Hello?" she called into the void.

More nothing.

If she moved back the way she came, it would be toward the gate, right? She'd return to where she started. She took one step, and then another, hands in front of her. When her surroundings stayed the same, she increased her pace until she was sprinting, then running at full-speed.

Still nothing. She pushed as hard as she could. Her lungs should be burning, her legs aching, but even those sensations were absent.

She pushed herself past what should be the point of collapse.

Frustration and despair sank in at the lack of shift in her environment. She wanted to kick something. Or punch it. Or do anything to interact the nothing around her. But that wasn't an option.

CHAPTER TEN

Cerberus had stepped through this gate more times than he cared to count, all in the name of assessing the situation and figuring out how to free Hades. It was like walking into another room. One that was endless miles of stone walls and a barren landscape of packed dirt.

This time, though, he expected to be grasping Lexi's hand when he did it. He frowned at the absence of her touch.

"Where is she?" Actaeon asked.

Tension coiled inside Cerberus. He glanced at the hero, but he was more focused on Lexi's absence. "I don't know." The muscles in his neck threatened to snap, despite the fact they weren't really there.

"Why the fuck not?" Actaeon's voice was low and threatening.

Cerberus let a growl rumble from his throat. Most of the time he could ignore Actaeon's attitude. With Lexi vanished into the literal void, he wasn't in the mood to take any shit. "Offer a solution or shut the fuck up."

Despite the lack of physical forms, he swore he could smell her scent, clinging to Actaeon. This wasn't helping.

"My solution? We go find her." Actaeon started walking away.

"Or we stay here and find her." Cerberus grabbed his arm and yanked him back. He didn't care about the glare directed at him. "She walked through the same gate we did, and she was holding my hand at the time. It stands to reason she's in the same place we are."

"So your answer is to sit here and wait for her to appear? This is why you're stuck in a dead-end job."

Cerberus racked his brain, trying to come up with next steps. His logic was solid, but he didn't like the idea of waiting on his ass for something to happen. "And driving a cab for the last thirty years is career advancement?"

"At least it's my choice."

"Uh-huh. Because doing things to spite someone—things you wouldn't do otherwise—is a big grand dose of freedom." Cerberus wouldn't be able to smell her or see her aura. Those things would manifest in his thoughts once they were here, but they would only be suggestions.

"I'm not serving anyone. That's what matters," Actaeon said.

Cerberus snorted. "But you do. You're a slave to what they don't want." This was something he never understood. He served Hades because Hades created him, and because Cerberus believed.

Actaeon was a mission-less soul, pretending he didn't care, for something stupid like not hearing his name used in the same sentence as a deity.

"Reverse psychology. Clever..." Actaeon trailed off with a frown.

"What?"

Actaeon looked at him, his scowl evaporating. "You didn't hear that?"

"No. What was it?" Cerberus would tease him about hearing voices, but down here, it meant someone was watching them.

"Nothing. Echoes from the past. Not real."

Except that if Actaeon heard it, whether or not it was real didn't matter. The illusion could manifest in other ways besides sound and become a real threat.

"*Cousin.*" A voice carried through the air.

Heracles. Cerberus' tension cranked beyond maximum capacity. Heracles could actually be real, given his allegiance to Zeus. Regardless, if he was a phantom of Actaeon's memories, he was just as dangerous, since Actaeon didn't believe Heracles could be beaten. Talk about being fucked.

Worse, if the real Hercules was guarding the entrance, there where greater obstacles beyond, so even if they made it past him...

This was double fucked with a pair of novelty dildos.

"Hey, Heracles." Actaeon's friendly tone was undercut by stress.

Heracles stopped a few feet from them. "Hades is in there for a reason."

"I'm not here for him," Actaeon said.

Cerberus kept his shock to himself. What did that mean? With the looming threat, it didn't matter. The physics down here were as familiar to him as breathing, and that single inhale was all it took for him to adopt his dog form. He wasn't a largish Doberman in here; he was a beast as tall as Heracles. He let out a low growl and stepped forward.

Actaeon glanced at him, a dry smile in place, then looked back at Heracles. "Two against one."

"I can't let you in."

"You know, gatekeeper is beneath you." Actaeon sounded casual, but his body tensed, and he rocked on the balls of his feet. His hands might be hanging limply at his sides, but there was a slight bend to his elbows and muscle rippled under his skin. "Tell you what. Give us back our traveling companion, point us toward the underworld, and we'll be on our way."

Cerberus was glad his frown didn't show. They weren't going to the underworld.

"There's no companion," Heracles said. "It's only the two of you."

"That's fine. We'll go through you, to get what we need." Cerberus spoke with far greater confidence than he felt, and lunged before the last word was out of his mouth.

"No, you won't." Heracles backhanded him without effort.

The blow landed across Cerberus' middle jaw and knocked him back several feet. If this was earth, his body would heal instantly. Here, the damage was to his soul, and the landing jarred that skull.

On third thought, they were triple fucked, with one of those large latex fists.

Actaeon shed his mask as well. He was no longer the slightly pale, any-man on the street. He looked like he was carved of marble and brought to life, with the permanent glint of moonlight.

Cerberus shook off the pain and stood. Actaeon's bow wouldn't do them any good against Heracles. The arrows wouldn't pierce his skin. Las Vegas proved that, in case anyone forgot.

It would be hand-to-hand combat, and Cerberus would be ineffective at dealing damage. But he could distract, and otherwise stay out of Actaeon's way.

Heracles was muscle, but Actaeon was speed. A punch thrown was dodged or blocked, but when it made contact, neither of them budged.

Cerberus darted forward, weaving in front of Heracles's legs. The walking bag of muscle landed a foot square in his gut, kicking him away again without breaking focus on the fight with Actaeon.

Cerberus swallowed past the burning agony in his midsection. He stumbled as he stood, but found his footing. If this was the only way to find out what happened to Lexi, he couldn't stay down. "Where is she?" he snapped out.

"Gone. Lost in the void." Heracles threw another punch at Actaeon, who ducked, rolled, and came up behind him with a fist to the kidney.

Heracles reached behind him, and grabbed Actaeon's wrist. With a twist, he flipped Actaeon, who landed on his feet, already sprinting away from another swing. It was a bluff. Heracles clipped Actaeon's jaw and sent him stumbling.

Cerberus latched onto the conflicting answer about Lexi, given that Heracles said Lexi wasn't here, when he arrived. Cerberus darted in again and clamped down on Heracles's leg with one head, and his side with another, using the third to keep an eye on their surroundings. His teeth didn't pierce the skin, but he was an obstacle.

Heracles grunted and tried to shake him loose, but Cerberus locked his jaws in place.

Actaeon landed a hit against Heracles' temple.

Heracles hissed, kicked Cerberus aside, and slammed him into the ground, inches away. Cerberus struggled to shake the stars from his thoughts. A foot headed toward a skull at high speed, and he rolled aside, a blink before Heracles stomped the packed dirt, where the head had been.

Neither hero looked winded. Instead, they were tense and flying at each other for another exchange.

Cerberus ached all over, and it had only been a few minutes. He didn't know how long he could keep this up—he couldn't compete with them. But he promised Lexi he'd keep her safe. He wouldn't fail her.

He bolted into the fray and was knocked aside like a fly, to land on his spine. The agony rocketed from all three heads down to his paws, and darkness clawed at the edge of his vision.

Actaeon could go through these motions all day. He grew up sparring with Heracles. While millennia altered both their fighting styles, the basic techniques stayed the same.

He couldn't win, though.

The cacophony of the past echoed in his skull—screams, the crunch of concrete and twisting steel, the whine of emergency sirens.

It mingled and sang off key until he wanted to scream.

There were no people here. It wouldn't be the slaughter Las Vegas was. He didn't have to hold back.

Not that it mattered. He hadn't held back before. The biggest difference this time was that when he slammed into the labyrinth wall, it held, rather than crumbling under the impact.

"You open to negotiations?" Actaeon forced out a levity he didn't feel.

Death Toll Unknown. The headline flashed in his thoughts.

Heracles shook his head and drove a shoulder into Actaeon's gut. "No."

Families Mourn for Bodies Never Found.

Actaeon couldn't shake aside the memories. "I don't want Hades. Cross my heart and hope you die."

"Heh." Heracles's laugh lacked humor. "Taking you with me."

Child of Moonlight Denounced by Zeus.

That one didn't hurt. Not directly. It was the scorn it earned Actaeon from those people he tried to help—the terror he saw in their eyes… It took more than a decade for most of them to forget.

Actaeon never forgot. Never forgave himself. "See? We have a common goal."

"What?" Heracles paused. His first hesitation since the fight began.

Actaeon took the opening and planted a sideways kick squarely in the back of his opponent's knee. "I want to get to the underworld. You're willing to sacrifice yourself to send me there. Let's cut to the chase."

Heracles stumbled but recovered in a flash. "You can apologize to every soul personally. It won't erase what you've done. You could have let it go."

He stepped forward, shaking the earth with this stomp. "Cassandra wasn't personal. She was a job."

"Fuck you." Rage surged cold and fluid inside Actaeon, until all he saw was a haze, filled with this arrogant, servile, unfeeling hero. Or was that his reflection? He swung as hard as he could.

And sent Heracles stumbling back.

The victory was short lived, as a fist collided with the side of Actaeon's head, jarring his brain.

"You only had to walk away. Before. Not after." Heracles's words drilled into him harder than any hit. "When she asked you to. Any time she asked you to. After she died. But you had to push it. You had to be the hero. You had to get vengeance. And then you gave up."

The words hit hard. The knuckles connecting with his throat at full speed hit harder. Actaeon gasped as the force of a freight train plowed into his windpipe.

He struggled to clench his hand. To swing back. But his muscles wouldn't cooperate.

CHAPTER ELEVEN

Lexi forced calm through her veins. Freaking out had never gotten her anywhere, and it wasn't the answer now.

She sat in the middle of the nothing, crossed her legs, and closed her eyes. Cerberus' instruction in meditation was little more than a crash course, but it gave her a starting point. Not that she had any idea what it would do for her, but it was the only prep she had for this place. Might as well give it a try.

She focused inwardly and tugged on a pleasant memory to help her relax. Things Dad used to tell her about Mom. The stories about them dating.

She slammed into a wall in her thoughts, and her head pounded in protest. What was there? She nudged, and agony spiked inside, making her gasp.

Her eyes flew open. Whatever that was, she needed to dig past it, but unless those missing two weeks of her life held some secret key to this place, this wasn't the time.

Lexi took one breath, and then another, talking herself through the process until the pain became a dull throb instead of a roaring inferno.

Meditation. She focused inwardly, on the strands of herself, and followed them. Unlike before, there was nothing else there. No Cerberus. No Actaeon.

That wasn't true. Ice and loyalty slipped into her thoughts. Two threads intertwined with hers but separate.

She didn't need to see past the illusion; she needed to become part of it. It sure would be nice to have that siren cuff right now. The faint tune of the earring hummed in her head. And then she heard something else. A grunt. A shout. Skin colliding with skin.

The nothingness became packed dirt. A stone wall stretched from one horizon to the other.

Cerberus flew straight at her, in dog form, but huge. Her heart jammed in her throat, but instead of colliding with her, he passed through her.

Actaeon stood a few feet away, looking like he had in the alley and trading blows with something she couldn't see. What was it? Her head pounded at the question, and she edged away from it.

"*Hello*?" she shouted.

Actaeon didn't turn. She spun toward Cerberus, who lay unmoving on the ground. A whimper bubbled up inside, and she ran to his side. She tried to rest a hand on his flank. If she focused, she could touch him instead of passing through him.

His chest heaved, but his eyes stayed shut.

"Cerberus?" She couldn't keep the panic from her voice.

In here, their auras were different; the ethereal light didn't so much glow, as weave with them. A faint red cord ran from her to Cerberus. Or was it to Actaeon? It danced and wavered, then vanished before she could tell.

"*Actaeon.*" She needed to get someone's attention. He was engrossed in his fight, and he didn't look good. His face was drawn, and he stumbled after each swing or step.

She stroked the hellhound's side, willing him to look at her. "*Cerberus.*" Why didn't they react to her?

Cerberus opened his eyelids to show narrow slits, then his eyes grew wide, and he focused on something behind her.

Something gripped her throat, cutting off air she didn't realize she was breathing, and lifted her off the ground. She kicked and clawed but didn't make contact with anything. Panic spilled inside, overpowering her thoughts and stealing what little breath she had left.

Cerberus thought he was hallucinating when he opened his eyes and saw Lexi kneeling next to him. When Heracles grabbed her by the throat and yanked her away, Cerberus shook off the fog of unconsciousness. She was the only thing that was real. Unfortunately, knowing that didn't make the rest of it vanish.

He propelled himself from the ground and latched onto Heracles' arms and shoulder, locking his jaws and willing his teeth to pierce flesh.

Actaeon slammed into Heracles, impacting him hard enough to knock him back and free Lexi from his grip.

She dropped to the ground with a grunt.

Cerberus was shaken loose as well, but he sprang back in without pause, looking for a way to distract Heracles. Zeus' champion was interested in Lexi now, ignoring Cerberus as though he were an insect.

Actaeon stepped in front of her. "You need to run."

"From what?" She wobbled and pushed to her hands and knees.

Cerberus swore the world slowed. There was no other way he could process everything he saw. Lexi stood, unsteady. Heracles drew within punching distance of her and Actaeon and twisted for an uppercut. Actaeon ducked, but Lexi grabbed his arm, interrupting his evasion and leaving him open to be hit.

Actaeon jerked his head in her direction, and Heracles's fist passed through him.

Cerberus watched in morbid fascination.

"I don't know what you see," Lexi said, holding Actaeon's gaze. "But I don't. There's nothing there."

Heracles vanished.

The pain Cerberus had held at bay surged in, eating at the edges of his vision until his world went black.

A light touch ran along his jaw to his ear, scratching and massaging. Cerberus forced away the fog in his brain and opened his eyes.

Lexi knelt next to him, watching him, her brows knitted together. She almost looked like Iris—a goddess of protection—in this light.

She let out a laugh of relief when she met his gaze.

He tried to move, but his heads were heavy. Plural? Right—he was in dog form. He willed his human shape into place and sat. "How long was I out?"

"Just a couple of minutes. How do you feel?" The concern in her voice warmed him, chasing away some of the aches.

Not the serious ones, though. He forced himself to ignore the pain. "I've been better." He looked past her to where Actaeon stood. "You've got some serious demons in your closet."

"Yeah. Sorry about that." Actaeon grimaced.

Lexi rested a hand on Cerberus' knee, drawing his attention again. The contact was pleasant. Almost enticing despite his condition.

"What happened?" she asked.

He considered using a *Harry Potter* analogy, but the last one earned him a blank stare. Apparently her dad didn't teach her about *all* of the classics. "When you put a trap in place that plays off people's darkest memories, and one of those is fighting the strongest hero in the world? This happens."

"There's a *strongest hero*? Who?" She looked puzzled.

"Heracles. Servant kiss-ass Number One of Zeus'?" Actaeon sounded exhausted.

Lexi cringed and pressed her palm to her forehead. "Never heard of him."

Actaeon gave a short laugh. "Tell me how you pulled that off, and I'll worship *you*."

Cerberus didn't see the humor in it. Lexi knew her history, and everyone learned who Heracles was. He was pretty sure she'd mentioned the name in their online chats. But he had bigger concerns right now. "Where were you?"

The look of pain vanished from her face. "Here. I think. I'm still having trouble seeing this place. I have to focus, to make out shapes. The ground. The maze."

"Because it's an illusion. All of it." Cerberus should have taken that into consideration.

"Cool." She hopped to her feet. "That makes things simple. We'll walk right through to our destination. Are you okay to stand?"

Cerberus wasn't the only one battered and bruised, but she wasn't hovering over Actaeon. Cerberus would be smug if his ego weren't wounded by failing at protecting her. "I'm good. I just need to walk it off." He stood, then waited for the world to stop spinning."

"I'm sorry." Actaeon sounded sincere.

Cerberus would give him a hard time about the apology or the events themselves, but this didn't seem like the time to be petty. "You couldn't have known, and I didn't have to ask you to join us." Technically, he didn't have a choice but to ask, since he was ordered by Hades, but Cerberus was supposed to keep that to himself.

"I'm not even here for your cause."

A motion out of the corner of Cerberus' eye caught his attention, and he glanced to the side to see Lexi shaking her head and scowling. The exchange with not-Heracles filtered back. "Then why are you here?" he asked Actaeon.

"I was bored." Actaeon shrugged.

Bullshit, times a million. Besides, Lexi's hunched shoulders and the way she watched her feet made him think there was more to it than that. It might be because she'd asked Actaeon to be here, but that seemed too simple.

Cerberus gave her his full attention. "Why are *you* here?"

"To free Hades—my father. That's why you sought me out. That's why I'm here. Daddy dearest and all that," she replied without missing a beat, but the words ran together.

She adored her stepdad and hated the gods almost as much as Actaeon did, which was why Cerberus thought she'd agreed to help. Hades would put a stop to all of it. Her answer didn't ring true, though.

"What's in the underworld?" Cerberus asked.

"Dead people." Actaeon smirked.

Lexi bounced on the balls of her feet. "Is this a pop quiz? I didn't study."

Great. They deflected conversation the same way. "Which dead person are you looking for?"

"Homer." Lexi had an answer ready. "I've always wanted to know why The Iliad doesn't match what we were taught in religious history."

"He was a corporate tool. Paid to write propaganda," Actaeon said.

The attempt to get him to think of anything else didn't work. Cerberus ticked through his thoughts to figure out what Actaeon could possibly want down here. What would have to do with Heracles and the underworld that would drag him from seclusion? That was it. What not-Heracles had plucked from

Actaeon's thoughts. Cerberus turned back to the hero. "Cassandra."

"Is dead." Actaeon's expression went blank.

"Dead or destroyed?" Once upon a time, Cerberus would have known, but when Hades was imprisoned, his servants lost administrative access to all the planes of death as well.

Actaeon's hesitation lasted a heartbeat too long. "Don't know, don't care."

"It's Mom." Lexi spat out. "She's been visiting me in dreams. She said if I came here with you, I could find her."

"Are you sure it was her?"

Lexi pursed her lips. "Yes."

Dizziness swept over him again, but not from the trauma of the fight. Was it possible? Persephone was back in the underworld? She was home?

CHAPTER TWELVE

Actaeon needed to move. Excess adrenaline mingled with decades-old guilt and made him twitchy. "Are you good to go?"

Cerberus nodded.

"Fantastic." Actaeon was trying not to be short with them which didn't come naturally. It was his past that caused the current delay, though. "Ask your questions while we walk. How do we get in?"

"There's an entrance about a thousand meters in that direction." Cerberus pointed.

"How do you know that?" Lexi asked. "If none of this is real, there's no guarantee the landscape is the same each time."

"Illusion isn't the same as *not real*." Cerberus brushed his fingers over the bruises on her neck.

A tinge of envy at the casually intimate gesture joined the disquiet churning in Actaeon, but he squashed it.

"And there's always an entrance about a thousand meters that way." Cerberus started walking.

Lexi didn't follow. "I can see through the walls. And whatever you two were hallucinating went away when I showed up…"

"Last time we walked through a wall with you, and it's only been about ten minutes, you disappeared," Actaeon said. The encounter with Heracles had him rattled. He needed to find his focus, before those skeletons cost lives again. Lexi's in particular.

The thought jarred him. Why did she have this kind of hold on his psyche?

"Last time, I couldn't see what was on the other side. Right now, I do. Isn't this why I'm here? Besides, I'd like to point out that I've given the two of you a lot more trust than most sane people would have. I think I deserve a little bit in return."

"She has a point," Actaeon looked at Cerberus.

Cerberus tangled his fingers with hers. "I'm trusting you. And I have no idea how this works, but I'd rather at least try and hold onto you to keep you from vanishing again."

"Makes sense." She smiled, and took Actaeon's hand as well. "I guess we're off to see the wizard?"

Old reference. Actaeon had to respect she'd been taught so much. "No yellow brick road, but as long as we stay away from the poppies, we'll be all right."

They stepped forward and walked through the wall. The next one waited about three meters away, and they strolled through that one without pause.

Maybe it really would be this easy.

"You never mentioned dreams," Cerberus said.

"That whole thing I just said about trust? I wanted to be generous, not stupid." Lexi kept her gaze focused ahead.

Actaeon winced at the brutal honesty.

"Do you trust me now?" Cerberus asked.

"It's been like… six hours. I don't know."

Actaeon wanted to be smug about her less-than-enthusiastic answer, but part of him felt bad for Cerberus. It was clear the guy had some sort of protective guard-dog puppy-love going on.

Lexi glanced at Cerberus. "You're still not telling me things."

"I'm telling you everything I can."

An interesting twist of words. Hades must be watching them more closely than Actaeon realized. Which made sense, that he would micromanage his own jail break.

"I'll give you details about the dreams," Lexi said with surrender, "but only because we're here, so we all need to know as much as possible." The edge of accusation grew in her tone.

That's your cue to spill, puppy. Actaeon kept the thought to himself. Calling Cerberus out wouldn't do anyone any good if staying silent wasn't his decision.

They had cleared at least five walls now. "Can you tell how many more are ahead of us?" Actaeon asked.

Lexi shook her head. "I don't see where they end. They fade into the mist after a point, and before that, they all overlap. Why can't I see Hades at the end of it all?"

Actaeon couldn't believe Cerberus hadn't explained this to her yet. "Don't think of an illusion like a hologram. Think of it as more of a pocket reality. That's as good a term for it as anything. You see this because we do. We can't see where Hades is. So if he's inside another illusion, you can't see him either. Like when you appeared in the middle of our fight."

"Thanks. That's as clear as anything around here." Sarcasm tinged Lexi's words.

"Tell me about the dreams. About Persephone," Cerberus said.

She told him the same story she'd told Actaeon. How her mother visited her in her sleep and said this was the way to pull her from the underworld.

Cerberus nodded through most of it. "Okay."

She raised an eyebrow. "Just like that?"

"You're willing to risk your life to be down here, and if that's why, I understand. You're walking through an illusion of a maze, with a hellhound and the son of Artemis. Who am I to question a series of dreams?"

If it were anyone else, the words would strike Actaeon as sarcastic, but Cerberus *was* a believer.

"He put me through twenty-times-five-billion questions." She gestured to Actaeon.

"You told him first?"

This was awkward to watch, but it was better for Actaeon than being in his own head.

"The woman with Mom said I should."

"Cassandra." Cerberus looked at Actaeon.

Actaeon shrugged. So much for steering clear of those memories. "Sounded like her, from Lexi's description." Lexi might be okay with spilling her guts, but he saw no reason to delve into the details of his conversation with Cassandra before she was killed.

Cerberus was silent. How much of this exchange was Hades involved in? Actaeon didn't expect an answer, so he didn't ask.

They stepped through another wall. How many was this? Twenty? More? He'd expected more trials. Not that he was complaining about the lack thereof. He stopped when he realized there was a small town in front of them, rather than another wall. He spun to find it behind them as well.

Let the fun begin.

It was like a Main Street in a city that didn't have much else, with buildings that could be fifty or even one-hundred and fifty years old. Each building was brick, with faded awnings, and vinyl lettering on huge plate-glass windows.

"I know this place." Lexi's tone had changed. It was lighter.

That could be good or very bad.

Cerberus walked ahead several feet, sweeping his gaze over shop fronts.

"I grew up around the corner." She pointed past the buildings. "Dad liked it because the infrastructure couldn't reach us. No cameras. Not enough people to make it worth the gods' time."

That wasn't right. Actaeon stretched his neck, but it didn't loosen the growing sense of ill-ease inside. "Faith can be massive in small communities like this. Gods don't leave that on the table."

"We had a temple of Aphrodite, but it was lip service." Lexi looked unconcerned. "They picked a neutral god, and that let them fly under the radar."

Cerberus returned. "Where's her temple?"

This didn't make sense. If Lexi only saw the illusions because they could, why would there be one created from her memories?

"End of the street." Lexi headed in that direction.

The closer they drew, the more Actaeon tensed. If she had pleasant memories of this place, why were they here?

They reached the one pristine building on the street, at the head of it all, like a proper temple. Unmarred stone steps led to a granite-faced building with columns supporting the overhang. Lexi walked forward and inside without hesitation.

Cerberus paused at the entrance with Actaeon.

Lexi whirled to face them. "Do you turn to ash if you step inside?" Amusement danced in her eyes.

"No." Actaeon forced down his doubts and followed her through the entrance. "But if it were a real temple of Aphrodite, she'd know we were here. So… habit."

"Like I said—lip service. She didn't care." Lexi wandered down the middle of the room.

The room was dotted with benches, made of the same polished marble as the building but with suede seat cushions. Plaster frescoes decorated the walls— images of Aphrodite and her most loyal maidens with worshippers in surreal and erotic dances.

It sure as fuck looked not only real, but also well-maintained.

Actaeon felt like he was going to crawl out of his skin. The illusion was so real, he could smell the lavender and orchids that meant Aphrodite had blessed this building.

Lexi should still be on edge. They were in the middle of an unknown place, and less than an hour ago, she'd watched the two men who were supposed to be the muscle in this operation get their asses handed to them by nothing.

The moment she stepped in the temple, her worry faded. Her childhood raced back, soothing her.

She stopped near the altar at the head of the room. It was more like a fainting couch, on top of a marble pillar. As a child, she thought that was cool. Now she had a feeling it was meant to be used for a more intimate but public kind of display.

That wasn't what drew her here, though. She ducked behind the marble, to the hollowed-out spot beneath. More suede cushions covered the floor, and several books were stacked in the corner. Exactly where she left them the last time she was here.

"I used to come in here as a kid and read." She grabbed the top book and stood.

"Read what?" Cerberus' question was strained.

She looked at the cover and the picture of Snow White. "Fairy tales." The less explicit version of what she found in Mom's books, a few years later.

Actaeon's face was pinched in a frown as he turned to Cerberus. "There's more to it than that. This isn't right."

"Agreed." Cerberus paced toward one of the walls and traced his fingers over the painting without making contact.

"It explains why no one knew where Lexi was. Did you send her here?" Actaeon asked.

Cerberus shook his head. "I had no idea where she was until recently."

She didn't care for the vague conversation. It should be because she was being left out. Logic screamed that in her head. The happy buzz said it was because they didn't like it here, but they should. "No cryptic bullshit I can't understand."

Actaeon looked at her again. "The temple is real. This is a house of Aphrodite. It means she knew where you were as a child, and was hiding you from everyone else."

This was ridiculous. "Why would any god do that for me?"

"I couldn't tell you." Cerberus' answer raked over her, scuffing her mood.

"Can't or won't?"

"Can't." He bit off the word.

Lexi flipped through the pages of the chapter book, letting the combination of story and the occasional picture fill in the gaps in her memory. "Right. Because the goddess of love would go out of her way to hide me—one of the keys to freeing Hades, the guy no one wants out. You're making me sound like some sort of Chosen One, and that kind of thing is total crap."

"Not crap. Fate," Cerberus corrected her.

"Not fate. Self-fulfilling prophecy." At least Actaeon saw it her way. "Someone decides you're important, and their actions make it true. How is this so real? So vivid?"

She didn't know. It was exactly like she remembered, but more vivid and detailed. It felt like home.

"Siren magic?" Cerberus asked.

Why were they still talking about the things that didn't matter? She wanted to show them how wonderful it was in here. A woman appeared behind them. One moment the spot was empty, and then it wasn't.

"Sirens can't do magic like this," the woman said.

Actaeon and Cerberus whirled, their bodies so tense, Lexi noticed from across the room.

"Dotty." Lexi smiled. The woman had been one of the few friends Lexi had as a child, who both glowed and didn't get mad at her for mentioning it. The pieces clicked in her mind, assembled by years of experience she didn't have back then. *Aphrodite.* "Oh."

"It's been a while." Aphrodite gave her a slight wave. "You look good. I didn't expect to find you here so quickly. But I'm glad you made your way to him." She nodded at Actaeon. "And this looks so real, because it is real."

That explained it. Lexi approached the group. The pleasant happiness wanted to linger, but this felt more important.

"How do you mean?" Cerberus asked.

"As in, really here." Aphrodite waved a hand, gesturing at the room. "I physically recreated the city

Alexandra grew up in, in the middle of the labyrinth."

None of this made sense on any level. Dad taught Lexi that gods couldn't make something from nothing. They'd like people to think they could, but they had to follow some basic rules. They could summon objects from other places. Reassemble them into something else. But it took a lot of power to even construct something as simple as a chair or a book. An entire city?

Why would anyone do that?

"How long did this take?" Actaeon asked.

Aphrodite made herself comfortable on one of the seats. Silken robes flowed around her as she crossed one knee over the other leg. "About twenty-five years. It wasn't my primary focus, you understand. I'd cart in the materials for a house one weekend, then come back and do a section of sidewalk the next."

"How do we get out?" Cerberus flickered, the image of a three-headed dog fading in and out over him.

"You don't. Not if you're trying to get to Hades." Aphrodite stood, strode to Lexi, and studied her. "There is an exit, and it's made just for you, but it will take you away from him. I love you, child, but you're not going near that fucking asshole or giving him a chance to get out of here. He'll kill us all."

The words sent ice down Lexi's spine. "I'm not trying to free him."

"I know"—Aphrodite trailed a finger along Lexi's cheek, leaving a disquieting combination of comfort and threat behind—"but that's what will happen."

"You couldn't have known twenty-five years ago that Lexi would be in the labyrinth." Actaeon's statement lacked conviction.

"No, but we planned for every possible occurrence when we made this place. And with the two of you, odds were high she'd come down here at some point. I didn't expect it so soon, but maybe I should have." Aphrodite searched Lexi's eyes. "The first time I saw you, the stunning little girl who saw right through me but didn't realize it, I knew what you were."

"What does that mean?" Lexi didn't like this talk of fate. She hated the idea that she didn't have any control over this situation. "Why not destroy me if I was a threat?"

"I don't want you dead. How cruel would that be? You have true love in your future, and I won't take that from you. When I met you, I saw those red threads of fate—at last two. And I realized who you were. I added this trial to the labyrinth in case you ever came for your blood father, and prayed you'd be content to stay away instead. You're not stuck here. If you want to go home, problem solved."

She made it sound so easy. Lexi liked the idea of *home*—not that she knew where that was. This city was the only place she'd ever called *home*.

"I envy you." Aphrodite sounded wistful. "But not the two of them." She kissed Lexi on the cheek. "Ciao." With that, she was gone.

"So we walk out of town," Actaeon said. "What's the quickest way out?"

Lexi dug through her memory and frowned. "I don't know."

"How can you not know?"

She clenched her jaw at the derision in his question. "We lived here until I was fourteen, and I didn't leave town in that time. When we moved, Dad woke me up in the middle of the night and said we needed to go. I was asleep in the car before we reached the end of the driveway. But it's not a big place. We walk in any direction, and we'll reach the edge. Just like magic."

He scowled. "Fine. Let's go."

The moment they stepped from the temple, Lexi's doubt returned full-force, reminding her this place, this situation—all of it sucked. She'd almost died earlier at the hands of nothing, because one of her traveling companions was suffering from the hero version of flashbacks.

They walked for a while, but the sun didn't seem to set here, so she had no idea how long. They passed the last of the houses and a fence surrounded by trees.

Then the housing grew denser again, and they walked back into town from the opposite side.

"Fuck." Actaeon's sharp tone dug deep, putting Lexi on edge.

They picked another direction, and then a third, with the results being the same each time. As they thought they were leaving the town, they walked back into it. Cerberus was limping, and Actaeon looked like he wanted to punch something.

Frustration clawed at her throat. Aphrodite said she knew how to get out, but Lexi had no idea. What were they supposed to do?

CHAPTER THIRTEEN

Cerberus could only think of one other time when the pain had lasted this long—when Hades let Morpheus punish him for letting Persephone escape.

This wasn't so severe, but the longer they traveled, the more he struggled to keep the anguish from his face. He'd recover if he could rest, but they needed to find a way out of here.

"We're not getting anywhere," Lexi said. She sounded dejected, her glee from when they arrived having faded hours ago. "We need a new approach."

"I agree." Cerberus had no idea what that was, though.

"We should go back to the temple." Lexi was already walking in that direction.

Actaeon planted his feet. "Were you listening to Aphrodite? That's *actually* her temple."

"And your point is?" Lexi turned a weary gaze on him. "If she had this town re-built here, the entire place is hers. At least the temple is comfortable. I want to sit." She looked at Cerberus, and her gaze softened.

"Let's rest." He was grateful she gave him the out.

Actaeon sighed. "Fine."

The moment they were back in the temple, Cerberus took one of the seats. Exhaustion spilled through him, and his limbs felt heavy. He was grateful for the breather, but it didn't mean they could stop looking for a solution. "We need to jog your memory. See what might feel like a way out."

Lexi sat next to him, hands on the seat, her arm pressed against his. She stared at her feet. "I was young. There are so many things that I see differently now. I'm happy to try, but I don't know where to start."

"Did you have any favorite hiding places?" Actaeon shifted his weight from one foot to the other, watching the doorway.

"The only place was behind the altar. I always liked it there."

Cerberus forced himself to relax. It was the only way he'd heal. The calm sinking into him helped. Aphrodite's influence. He could see why Lexi liked it then and why she was drawn to it now.

"Maybe it's not about Lexi directly. Persephone is the key to the underworld," he said.

"But not the key to wherever this is." Actaeon gestured toward the doorway.

Lexi kicked one foot back and forth. "Copperton, Utah."

She was stunning. Even in this unnatural light from an unknown source, she was beautiful.

"What did you do here as a kid, for fun?" Cerberus asked.

"Nothing. Or rather, nothing unusual. I climbed trees. I read—a lot. I watched Dad's old movies and played video games."

"Did you play hide and seek?" Cerberus figured, if she had any favorite hiding spots, getting out of here might be related.

"No. My dad would tease me about falling in Narnia if I wasn't careful. And I never did that Platform Ten-Sixths thing either."

Cerberus stared at her blankly, trying to decipher the words. "Platform Nine and Three Quarters? From Harry Potter?"

"Is that what it's from? No wonder I didn't recognize it." Lexi laughed. Such a sexy sound. "Never picked it up."

"Wait. Your stepfather taught you about Star Wars and Narnia and how to defeat a beholder, but you don't know Harry Potter?"

She shrugged. "He said I wasn't a muggle, so there were more important things for me to learn."

Cerberus shook his head, but the logic was its own kind of *so wrong it's right*. "I'll have to introduce you when we're done here."

"I don't know what you two think is so awesome about this… whatever you're doing, but we can't sit around here and wait." Actaeon looked like a tightly-bound bundle of stress.

Lexi stifled a yawn. "I know you big, badass immortals don't need your sleep, but I still haven't figured out that trick, and I was running near empty when we got here. Besides, we don't have a direction."

"A few more hours won't make a difference one way or the other." And it would give Cerberus time to find his strength. Besides, he was worried about pushing Lexi so hard.

"I don't like it here." Actaeon flexed his fingers. "It makes me feel…" He shook his head. "I'm going to see if we missed something. A way out that's not trapped. Somewhere. Stay here, take it easy, and I'll be back."

Actaeon left, and Cerberus stopped fighting the weariness. It didn't matter that Actaeon was currently an ally; his general abrasive attitude set Cerberus on edge.

"Do you think you'll be able to sleep?" he asked Lexi.

"I don't know, but my brain needs to relax." She hopped from the bench. "The cushions under the altar are loose. I'll be right back."

He watched her jog to the front of the room, studying the way her jeans hugged hips that swayed with each step. Lust spiked inside. He knew better than to let such a base instinct overwhelm him, but in here it was hard to ignore.

The one upside to this, he couldn't hear Hades in Aphrodite's temple.

She returned with an armful of cushions and arranged them on an empty bit of floor a few feet away. She sat and patted the spot next to her. "Join me? I'm not the only one who's exhausted."

"I guess." He exaggerated his reply. "But only if you try to rest."

She lay on her side, the corners of her mouth tugging up playfully. "All right."

He lay beside her, facing her. The light dimmed to pleasant. In here, it was easy to forget what was beyond the temple walls.

Especially when she caught her bottom lip between her teeth, amusement dancing in her eyes. "What?" she asked.

"When I was sent to find you, I never expected *you*."

"I don't understand."

"Witty. Stubborn. Beautiful."

Her smile turned shy. "Surprise?"

"The best kind." He brushed her hair off her face and neck, exposing the mark of Death. He traced his fingers along the outline of the familiar shape.

She tilted her head, giving him better access, and her lips parted in a silent sigh. "I'm surprised you can see that. Didn't I leave it behind with my body, like the earring?"

"It's part of your soul." The contact raced through him, tugging at desire. "Every hero has one, but most don't choose to reflect them in ink."

"I didn't know what I was doing. I was young, and it felt like the thing to put there." She licked her lips.

He wanted to lean in and kiss away the shine. A tiny bit of him knew the impulse was out of place in the midst of the madness they were trapped in, but more of him thought it felt right. As though he'd been denying the need pulsing inside for the last several days, and now it was all right to acknowledge it. "You wear it well."

"Do you have one?"

He tugged down the collar of his shirt, to expose the brand a few inches below his collarbone. "Mine's a little different. It binds me to the god I serve." It was intertwined with his soul, all the way to the core.

"Mine doesn't?"

"No." He couldn't picture her bowing down to anyone.

"What if you didn't want to serve?" A frown whispered across her face. She pressed her palm to his mark.

He sucked in a sharp breath at touch. "It's not as easy for me to walk away as some people would try to convince you it is." He didn't want to say Actaeon's name. It might break the spell wrapped around them. "You were born. I was created. I cease to exist if I refuse to serve. If I didn't follow Hades,

I'd have to find someone else worthy of my services."

"I like that you phrase it that way. Does he deserve you?"

"Yes." Cerberus had no doubt. "I've followed Hades to the ends of the earth and back, and will again." He let impulse guide him and leaned in to brush his lips over hers.

She pulled away with a frown, and his heart sank. "You should know something," she said.

He had to strain to hear the words. Without asking, he realized what her confession was. "I already do." The scent of sex that bothered him earlier, the disconcerting combination of her smell with Actaeon's that gnawed at him, didn't matter now. "You slept with him."

"No. He bent me over the sink and fucked me. There was no sleeping. No intimacy." The way she said it, the words were neither good nor bad. They just were.

Cerberus drew a finger up her arm, reveling in her gasp. "I'm not blind. Something connects the two of you."

"Yes. But it's there with you, too."

"No one expects immortals to be monogamous, especially so early in life." And it wasn't as though fated mates were a thing for anyone but humanity, regardless of what Aphrodite thought she saw. He didn't need to jade Lexi with that thought though. His reluctance to say it had nothing to do with the bitter taste it would leave in his mouth.

"I'm not exactly looking to go tasting every immortal fruit out there. Wait. I didn't mean that the way it sounded."

He grasped her fingers and raised them to kiss along the tips. Why did that feel so right? "I got what you meant." He cupped the back of her neck and crushed his mouth to hers.

The kiss silenced the nagging voice in the back of his mind that insisted this wasn't the time. That there was something off about the circumstances. When Lexi pressed her body to his, he said *fuck it* to the rest of the world.

Right now, nothing else existed.

CHAPTER FOURTEEN

The pull Lexi felt to Cerberus was overwhelming. Sparks of desire raced through her when he slid his hand up her chest, between her breasts. This wasn't the frantic get-off-now from the bar. It was slow, seductive, and necessary. An overwhelming compulsion to be closer to him. To feel everything. To fall into each other's pleasure and not resurface until they were beyond spent.

Clothes fell away quickly. She didn't know who removed what, but the need to feel his skin against hers drove her actions. Everything was painted with vibrancy, and she wanted experience as much as possible while riding this high.

And then Cerberus' mouth was everywhere—gliding down her neck, sliding over her nipples as he paused to suck and lick, and then moving lower. When he drove his tongue between her legs, seeking out her core, she gasped and arched her back, pressing into his touch.

She wanted to fuck, hard and fast. And she wanted to spend hours making love. And she wanted everything in between. Desire stole any other thought but how good it felt to be with him.

Climax rolled through her, and she dug her nails into his back, holding him in place until her orgasm ebbed.

He rolled onto his back, pulling her on top of him, and thrust inside her. Their connection wasn't physical, though she felt every touch. His essence mingled with hers, twirling and intertwining. When he spilled inside her, it was more than release; it was completion.

She shuddered as the climax faded away, and felt an odd absence when he slid out of her. She rolled to lie next to him and rested his head on his chest.

Cerberus pulled a blanket over them. She had no idea where it came from, but it kept them wrapped together, and she was desperate for that right now.

"Ahem."

Lexi forced her eyes open at the exaggerated sound of someone clearing their throat, to see Actaeon seated on a nearby bench. She hadn't meant to fall asleep.

"Glad you got some rest," he said dryly. "What if I wanted to watch?"

Cerberus tightened his grip around Lexi's waist.

She couldn't tell if Actaeon was joking or serious or upset. The haze in her head made her want it to be a sincere statement, but with him here, so close, it was as though the unnatural drive was muted. His presence subdued the drug-like high in her veins. Not as though he erased her desire, but he smothered the irresistible compulsion behind it. "Did you have any luck?" she asked.

"Not as much as you." This time the sarcasm was distinct.

What gives you the right? The question popped into her head, bouncing against hurt and guilt she didn't think she deserved. "Don't."

"I'm sorry." He sounded surprisingly sincere. "I found a house. A lot of them, obviously, but one has pictures of Persephone, and I assume mini-you."

She sat up, holding the blanket over her chest. An odd conflict raged inside, modesty arguing with the voice insisting it wasn't needed with them. "Little pink ranch with two bedrooms and an ugly-ass tile job in the kitchen?"

"That's the one."

"That's home. I want to see."

"I'd show you where it is, but you probably already know."

She nodded. "Let us get dressed, and we'll go."

"I'm waiting," Actaeon said.

"Well, turn around."

He rolled his eyes and turned away. "I'll be outside."

Cerberus sat up behind her and kissed along her bare shoulder. It helped quiet the uncertain half of her mind. "How are you doing?" he asked.

"Good." Bad. Confused. She wanted to lean back into him. Her desire to fuck again sucked the air from her lungs. She turned her head to the side, to steal a kiss.

He cupped her breast, swallowing her groan. "I bet we have a little time before he comes back," he murmured against her lips.

It was so tempting. "No." She pulled away, and it felt like something inside snapped. A spell, broken. "We should go."

He stared at her blankly, before his expression shifted to something sterner. "You're right."

They dressed in silence, keeping their distance, then joined Actaeon.

The moment she stepped outside, the haze lifted from her mind. Overwhelming lust faded to a whisper begging for a touch, and then it was gone. A new feeling of disquiet set in. The memories of last night were still pleasant, but they were more like she watched them from a removed perspective.

A shiver raced over her. It was as if the temple violated her.

You didn't do anything you didn't want to.

That was true, but it didn't mean it was a good idea. She didn't—couldn't—blame Cerberus. Whatever drove her overtook him as well. But she didn't like the creeping feeling that she'd been out of control.

And Actaeon blocked it. Not removing her desire, just the unnatural compulsion.

Uncomfortable silence settled between the three as they walked toward her childhood home. She wanted to break through the quiet, but nothing seemed appropriate.

They reached the little pink cottage and stepped inside. It was what she remembered but *more*. A vivid picture, where her memories were faded. Photos lined the walls and mantle. Of her growing up. With Dad. By herself. And then there were the images of Mom.

Cerberus stopped in front of one, tracing his finger along the glass. The longing and sadness on his face stole her breath and squeezed her heart.

"You loved my mother." The words surprised her, but they tasted true. An ache grew behind her ribs. Was he only with Lexi because he couldn't have Mom?

"Yes." His voice was quiet.

That didn't make her feel any better.

Cerberus looked at her. "Not in the way you're thinking. Persephone was my queen. I served her because I wanted to. Because her kindness deserved loyalty, and she was more of a goddess than any I've ever met, despite being born mortal. But there was no romance. I never wanted intimacy or affection of any similar type of relationship."

At the assurance, Lexi's hammering heart quieted. "Was she really that good?"

"She really was." Actaeon's voice startled her.

She'd almost forgotten he was here.

"We should look around," he said. "See if anything triggers a thought or gives you a hint as to what Aphrodite was talking about."

"All right." Lexi didn't expect to find anything, though. It was a small home. Searching it didn't take long. Everything personal was on display. There were no clothes in the dressers or closets. No food in the pantry. All the drawers, cabinets, and shelves were bare.

She was still having trouble with the passage of time here, but she doubted it took more than fifteen minutes to go through the place. They stood in the living room again, no closer to answers than when they arrived.

"I can't believe she got every detail right." Lexi wished they could stay. Not that moving into an empty town in the middle of a magical maze was smart, but the comfort of this place was impossible to ignore.

Actaeon raised an eyebrow. "That ancient artifact of a game console in the armoire in the master bedroom is real? That thing was old before you were born."

"That's up there?" She couldn't fight her grin. "I used to play Spiro the Dragon over and over. I sucked, but I loved it." The memory swelled inside, carried on familiarity, and she let out a sad laugh before she realized she'd done it.

"What are you thinking about?" Cerberus's tone was concern mixed with wonder.

A pit of bittersweet tinged the past. "There were times when I wasn't allowed to go outside. Looking back, Dad was probably hiding me. All I knew then was that I was bored and felt trapped. I'd crawl into the wardrobe and pretend it was my door to Narnia."

Cerberus stared at her. "Want to go give it one last glance?"

She almost swore he could read his thoughts. It couldn't be that easy, could it? Actaeon already checked inside. But whatever Aphrodite put in place wasn't meant for him.

"Yes." Lexi sprinted up the stairs, hearing two sets of footsteps follow. She paused in the doorway to her father's bedroom, her heart jamming in her throat. It was so much him. The dragon mural on one wall. The swords hanging opposite the painting.

And the wardrobe, across from the bed.

She had to will her feet to move forward. She didn't know which would be more disappointing— opening the door and finding what had always been there, or finally discovering it lead to another place. One that wasn't home.

She traced her fingers over the intricate carving, took a deep breath, and grasped the brass knob. When she tugged the door open, she swore her heart stopped.

Instead of a back wall, she saw a dirt path, lined with trees.

"What is it?" Cerberus asked.

Of course. She was the only one who could see through the illusion. "A way out."

She grasped their hands, and stepped through.

And then the house was gone. They were in the labyrinth again.

Home was gone. Sadness settled in. So did something else. The air felt different here. Suffocating and tangible. Their surroundings were as solid as in the city Aphrodite built.

"*Fuck.*" Cerberus' shout jarred her.

Actaeon stepped in front of him, half blocking Lexi. "Whoa. Chill."

Cerberus scrubbed his face. The frustration spilled from him. "We're not in the labyrinth anymore. We're at the edge of the underworld." He nodded at a river just at the edge of their visual range. "That's Styx."

"We could go see Mom?" Lexi's hope returned, laced with hesitation, but strong. "That is, I know you have your goal, or orders, or whatever, but... we're here anyway."

"I vote yes," Actaeon said.

"Of course you do." Cerberus's scowl etched lines in his face. "I have no clue what else we're going to do, so sure."

"Don't sound so enthusiastic." Lexi bit off the sarcastic retort.

Cerberus' expression softened. "I'm sorry. I would like to see her again."

As if that was enough consensus, they all started walking toward the water. Silence settled between them, punctuated by the scuff of their feet on the dirt.

"How did Persephone die?" Cerberus' question startled her and did nothing to help her scattered thoughts. "I'm sorry for asking. I wish I didn't feel compelled to know."

"She—" Lexi's head throbbed, and she winced. "I don't know. I was a baby." The pain ebbed, but only slightly. She nudged the patch of fog in her brain, and it pulsed behind her eyes.

"Your dad never told you?" Actaeon asked.

She shook her head. "I guess not."

Quiet descended over them again. This was oppressive. "How did Cassandra die?"

"Heracles killed her," Actaeon said softly. "Because I pissed off Zeus."

"I'm sorry."

"Me too." He spoke through clenched teeth.

"I probably shouldn't ask, but is that why he was outside the maze? That's who you said it was, didn't you? Heracles?"

She couldn't interpret the look Cerberus gave her, beyond the fact that it didn't look happy.

Actaeon let out a long breath. "Him being there probably had more to do with what came after Cassandra. When I found him in Las Vegas."

Her head pounded again, and she pressed her palm to her forehead. "I take it that didn't go well?"

"*Las Vegas.*" Cerberus emphasized the words. Like that would make her understand them differently. "As in, The Battle of Las Vegas?"

Agony threatened to split her skull in two, and she stumbled.

Both men stopped, and Cerberus wrapped an arm around her waist, catching her.

She forced herself upright. "I'm okay."

Actaeon didn't look convinced. "It was a horrible fight. Heracles and I… It was bad."

"It was about the time you were born." Cerberus was studying her like she might break at any minute. The pain said it might be true. "You wouldn't remember it from the news, but they teach it in schools."

A barrier shattered in her head. A screeching threatened to rupture her eardrums, and an onslaught of images flooded her mind. The rush made it impossible for her to unjumble them, and she dropped to her knees with a gasp.

Cerberus was by her side in an instant, reaching for her. She shoved him away. There was already too much. His touch was one more thing she couldn't process.

Two weeks of her life, no longer missing. Two weeks of scattered sleep and the siren who looked like Lorelei but wasn't. Of the music, soulful and deep. Of the voice telling her what to forget, over and over, before depositing her on a street corner in New York.

It wasn't a generic voice though. It was Aphrodite.

"I'm sorry to do this to you, child." The familiar voice hammered against Lexi's skull. *"If you remember Persephone's past, it will keep you from a true love. I need you to forget Las Vegas long enough to give him a chance."*

The stories Dad told her as a child slammed into her. About what happened to Mom. That two selfish, indiscriminate heroes took their petty squabbles to the streets, causing so much death in the process. Including Mom's.

She gasped through the pain and forced herself to look at Actaeon. "It was you."

"What was?" His frown was deep.

"You fucking bastard." She poured the venom into her words and willed her agony onto him. "You killed Persephone. You and Heracles took my mother from me."

CHAPTER FIFTEEN

Guilt clawed its way through Actaeon, stifling his thoughts and squeezing the breath from his lungs. "No. Persephone wasn't in Las Vegas. She wouldn't place herself in a place with so many cameras."

When Lexi pushed to her feet, her grimace stretched her face. She gasped and squeezed her eyes shut, holding her head with both hands. The air stilled, as if waiting for her to act. She focused on him. "She was. All three of us were. Dad was a blackjack dealer at The Luxor. Said it was best to hide in plain sight."

The pain faded from her face as she spoke, replaced with fury. "And then you and that asshole lapdog of Zeus'—" She glanced at Cerberus. "No offense."

"Some taken." Cerberus reached for her.

She brushed his hand away with a scowl. "I'm fine."

"I know it hurts." Cerberus' voice was kind. "But Persephone didn't die. You've seen it. That's why you're here. This allowed her to return home, to sit on her throne in the underworld. Unless the soul is destroyed, it moves to a new plane of existence."

Lexi turned a narrow-eyed glare on him. "A home she was shackled to even after she fell out of love with Hades. The place she ran from when she had the chance. Except, this time, she wasn't taken with her body, so she's a lot more bound to it than she was before. Don't you dare fucking tell me this is for the best."

"I'm not."

Actaeon couldn't listen to this. Not with his own thoughts assaulting him. How many others who were important to him, to her, to people he cared about had died? Not that it mattered. Everyone he killed, regardless of his intent, was important to someone. Guilt scooped out an empty cavern in his chest that he did this to Lexi, but it was a reminder of how many people his actions impacted.

This was his chance to witness the pain firsthand.

"And don't you take his side." She pointed to Actaeon. "He can topple buildings with a fucking bow and arrow. I've seen the video. He doesn't need you to defend his actions."

Cerberus shook his head. "I'm not. Trust me. One thing I won't do is tell you Actaeon deserves understanding. But it's not the end of the world."

Any other day, and Actaeon would have snapped back with an insult. "Don't celebrate

Persephone's death. You can't honestly be trying to justify this. I did reckless, horrible things. Things that can't be taken back."

"Don't you dare." Lexi whirled on him and forced her words through clenched teeth. "You haven't earned the right to wallow in self-pity over this."

"That's the last thing I'm doing."

"That's the *only* thing you're doing. It's the only thing you've done since it happened." Venom dripped from her words.

"It's guilt. I was wrong." He couldn't believe he was defending himself for hating his own actions. What was happening?

She slammed her palms into his chest and shoved him, catching him off guard. He stumbled back a step.

"You fucking asshole," she spat. "You killed people, and that sucks massive fucking donkey balls. Or they died because of your negligence. Semantics, I suppose. Except that's the problem—either way, they're dead."

"I'm not arguing—"

"And I'm not done. Instead of making sure more lives weren't lost by the hundreds, by the thousands, you turned your back on all of it. You went and sulked on the sidelines. Sure, you offer up the occasional pity rescue. Some poor unfortunate human gets in the way of a gargoyle, and you step in with a conveniently placed arrow. Like rescuing a kitten from a tree. You're such a big, important hero. But that doesn't address what lies at the heart of the fucking issue."

Actaeon stared at her, struggling to find a response. "You want me to fight *more*? To potentially make things worse?"

She shoved him again, but this time he was prepared. Her palms slapped against his shoulders, and she stalled. Her growl rivaled Cerberus'. "Stop pouting in the corner like a spoiled child who had his wrist slapped. Get off your fucking ass and change things."

"People *died*. Thousands." Was he speaking a different language? What didn't she understand about the severity of The Battle of Las Vegas?

"Thousands die anyway. Poseidon took two-hundred and fifty for solstice a few days ago. He forced a family to choose between their only daughter and her two-year-old son. They chose for the boy to live, she pleaded for her own life, so he killed the son and family and granted her appeal." Lexi didn't sound like she'd be running out of steam anytime soon.

"In three months, he'll do it again. Maybe he'll only want one-hundred next time, but perhaps it will be one-thousand. And he's done this every celebration for the last fifty years. So has Zeus. And Ares. And others. So stow your self-loathing, stop picking on Cerberus for at least having the balls to pick a side, and—"

Lexi vanished. Like bad editing in an old movie, one frame she was there, and the next she wasn't. Cerberus wasn't there either.

Actaeon stood alone at the edge of Styx, trees and dirt stretching in one direction, and water in the other, as far as the eye could see.

"Lexi?" he said. "*Lexi,*" he shouted. "*Cerberus.*"

The landscape didn't even afford him the kindness of echoing his voice back at him.

Lexi's accusation pounded in his skull, but now wasn't the time. Did she slip outside of the illusion, like when they'd arrived? If so, why was Cerberus missing too?

And who the fuck did she think she was, telling him he wasn't helping any? Snotty little brat who'd decided she had a grip on the world, with less than half a century under her belt?

You know she's right.

He knew she was missing, and the scratching need to find her overpowered anything else. He couldn't do nothing.

That's what you've been doing all along. Lexi's voice bounced in his head.

Now wasn't the time.

It never is.

He had to get her back. The urge was so potent, nothing else mattered. He forced focus through his veins, needing a direction. A plan of action.

His nose twitched. What was that smell?

Centaurs.

Dangerous. Vicious. Predatory. Answering to no one. And if they had Lexi…

Fuck. This was bad.

Cerberus was getting tired of waking up with a pounding headache. He expected to face trials in here, but this was ludicrous.

When he opened his eyes, darkness stared back. He lifted a paw in front of his face, but couldn't see it.

Paw? This wasn't right. None of his heads could see anything. Why was he in dog form? He willed himself to shift back to human. Three heads still weighed heavily on his shoulders.

Why couldn't he change? *"Lexi? Actaeon?"*

No response. They'd been arguing. More like she was yelling. The last few minutes before unconsciousness rushed back. She was upset at Actaeon. Not because he'd killed Persephone in Las Vegas—though apparently he did—but because of the way he withdrew after.

Cerberus would almost feel pleased about her anger. Proud that she was taking the stand she was. Infatuated with the gorgeous, bold beauty, shouting at one of the world's most powerful heroes, at the top of her lungs, to stop being a baby.

Given the circumstances, which he couldn't define, celebration would wait.

He forced himself to stand. That didn't seem to be an issue. His legs worked fine. His paws rested on solid ground. It was body temperature, and smooth like polished stone or concrete.

He sniffed the air. Magic teased him, but it was faint. Nothing potent enough for him to identify. He padded forward slowly, heads searching, and ran into a set of bars.

He passed a paw along the iron. The bars were so close together he could fit a toe through, but not much else. He followed the wall to one corner, and then three more. The box wasn't big. Maybe three or four times his hound form. He couldn't discern any break in the pattern. No obvious door.

He tried to climb, but there was nothing to dig his claws into.

He braced himself for the pain, backed up against one side, and charged full force into the opposite wall. His shoulder screamed in revolt when he slammed into the prison bars.

He tried several times, gritting his teeth through the pain, but his joints couldn't take much more. He'd bruised himself to the point his leg screamed in agony when he put weight on it. And he hadn't felt anything give in the prison.

He sat on his haunches. What now?

A faint glow crept up the edges of his vision. Was he seeing stars? Had he done that much damage to himself?

He followed the source of light to a string of characters on the ground outside the bars. As the glow grew brighter, he could make them out. Greek. A binding spell. It was keeping him in the cage and in his dog form.

His eyes adjusted as the light in the room grew to from nothing to dim. Being able to see didn't offer any additional information.

The scent in the air shifted. He knew this one. It was like Lexi, but minus the traces of Hades and Persephone.

"Cerberus." Cassandra stepped into his line of sight. "I'm sorry about this."

That ought to make Actaeon happy. Or piss him off more, since the whole death-of-thousands thing had been vengeance for her. "What is *this*?"

"A cage. Built for you."

So much for asking questions. He was going to try a couple more anyway. "Where's Lexi?"

"Doing so much better than either of you. What do you see in her?"

Lexi was intelligent, willful, stunning, driven… The list came easily, but he wasn't willing to share. "Color me not reassured."

"You have to stay in here. Possibly forever, though I'm not certain yet. I'm uncertain about so many things these days." She gave a strained laugh. "It's all so fuzzy."

"Why are you here?"

"Because," she said. "Because, because, because. I used to hate knowing what would happen next. Now I'd give so much to see it. There are so many threads. Not for you. For the world. It's so hazy. But Actaeon is supposed to come for me, and he won't if you're not here. I tried to tell Persephone that was the real reason to bind you. No one ever believes me, though. Do you?" She looked at him, her gaze heavy with sadness.

Cerberus wasn't sure how to respond. Hades would kill, but only those necessary. That was his plan. Where was he? Why couldn't Cerberus hear him? "I believe you."

"Yeah, no." Cassandra turned away.

"Wait. I need to get out. I need—"

"To get to Lexi? To Hades? She's not worth your time, and he'll find you when he needs." She gestured to the characters on the floor. They were fading again. Sapping the light from the room. "The wards will bind you here, slowly severing your link with Hades. You'd better hope he wants you loose soon. Otherwise when the bond is broken, you'll be mortal. Without a body, you won't age, but your mind rapidly will. You'll creep toward insanity as his ambient power seeps away, until only traces of your mortal soul are left. And when it's devoured you from the inside-out, you'll cease to exist."

"No, no, no." Cerberus couldn't keep the panic from his voice. He couldn't abandon Lexi. Wouldn't. "He wouldn't want me here you know that."

Cassandra's sad smile twisted. "I do know that. And so much more. The things he's told me… Goodnight, Cerberus."

The wards faded, and her scent vanished.

"Cassandra."

Nothing.

Cerberus summoned all his strength and charged the walls of his prison again and again. He couldn't stay in here. He wouldn't.

CHAPTER SIXTEEN

"…stop picking on Cerberus for at least having the balls to pick a side, and…" Lexi trailed off mid-rant, when the labyrinth vanished, along with her traveling companions.

"No. Fuck this. You're not taking this away from me." She didn't know who she was talking to, but given the nothingness around her, this was similar to the situation when they'd arrived. She'd been moved to a different layer of space than her companions, and needed to get back to them.

Before she could find the right words to protest, her arms jerked back, jarring her shoulders and sending a spike of discomfort through her. Something rough bit into her wrists, and then her ankles.

"I'm sorry, daughter of Death." A voice came from behind.

"Not this again. I am so sick of being labeled by…"

A man stepped into view. Correction—he had a man's torso and a horse's body. Sick dread welled inside Lexi. According to history, centaurs were sadistic and lewd, and only interested in kidnapping and rape.

"What would you prefer I call you?" he asked.

Lexi's anger faded behind dread. "Whatever you'd like." No reason to antagonize him. Her mind whirred a million miles a minute, and she tried to sift panic from plotting.

"*Alexandra*? Like a proper oracle? *Lexi*, like your stepfather called you? I'm Chiron, by the way. It's a pleasure to meet you."

How did he know so much about her? "*Lexi* is fine."

He strode toward her, and she tried to back up, but her bound feet made her stumble and land on her ass.

"I'm sorry for the restraints." He sounded kind enough. Was that part of some fucked-up mind game? "I need you to come with me, and this is a no-negotiation kind of thing, but I'm not going to hurt you. The ropes will come off as soon as we reach our destination."

"Which is…?" As a child she'd been taught never to go with the kidnapper. Never let them take her away from people. That didn't seem applicable here.

"I can't say. I wish I could. But it won't take us long."

"I'm good here, thanks." She scooted away on her butt, and he matched her attempted escape with slow, plodding steps.

"You'll understand soon enough, and I promise you won't be disappointed."

She chuckled nervously. "You'll forgive me if I have a hard time taking your word for it."

Chiron nodded. "Sleep."

Lexi's world went black.

"Take the ropes off her." A woman's voice drilled into Lexi's thoughts.

It was soothing and familiar, like home wrapped in love. Lexi opened her eyes, surprised there was no grogginess. The bindings on her wrists and legs fell away. She stood, rubbing the rope burns as she took in her surroundings. It was a simple room. A couch, a few chairs… It looked straight out of an IKEA catalog, circa twenty-twenty-eight.

"I'm sorry about the theatrics. Everyone is watching you right now."

Lexi spun toward the voice, to find a woman about her height watching her, adoration on her face. Lexi's only memories of this person were from photos and dreams, and neither did her justice. "Mom?"

"Alexandra." Persephone opened her arms.

Lexi shook her head and stepped back. "No. How do I know it's you?" She wanted it to be. Inside her, a little girl screamed to walk into the hug.

"That's a fair question. I'd say you don't, but *you* do. You can see that it's me."

Logic warred with the events of the past few days. "Why didn't your centaur friend—"

"Chiron," Persephone said.

"—just tell me this was where he was bringing me? You said if I went into the labyrinth, you'd be there. I've been wandering for more than a day. Why now? How can I trust any of this?"

"Chiron couldn't tell you, because as I mentioned, everyone is watching you." Persephone held up a finger. "And it took us a while to get you, because you vanished from the labyrinth shortly after you appeared." She ticked off a second finger, as if counting down a list. "And whether or not you trust any of this is up to you, but you can ask me anything, and I'll answer. Did I get all of them so far?"

Lexi sank onto the couch, trying to straighten her thoughts. It felt real. Could she trust her instinct? It didn't generally steer her wrong, but she didn't know the rules in this place. "Where are we?"

"The underworld. My corner of it."

That didn't ring true. "I thought you were queen here. Why don't you have a palace? Are you living modestly to keep the *plebes* from revolting?"

Persephone laughed. "You don't really ask one thing at a time, do you? I do't rule anymore because Hades doesn't. And plebes, really? Tell me you don't believe I think like that."

"No." Unless every person they'd ever known in common was stupid—and that wasn't the case—Persephone wasn't a *look down on people* kind of ruler.

"May I ask *you* something?" Persephone said.

Lexi nodded, her brain too muddled for her to refuse.

"Where have you been? Or rather, what happened to you after you arrived?"

"Aphrodite," Lexi said. "We were in a recreation of the town Dad and I moved to, after you—Mom-you?—died."

"That makes sense."

"It does? How does *any* of this make sense?"

Persephone perched on the edge of the chair across from her. "No one knows all the traps that keep Hades in the labyrinth, but I can see why Aphrodite would be involved. It's complicated, but it's not. I can explain it all, but first I need to know you're not going to let Hades out."

"I don't give a fuck about the gods. I'm not here for him; I'm here for you." And for Cerberus. And Actaeon. "Where are my traveling companions?"

Persephone grimaced. "No one fucks with Actaeon. Did they explain that to you?"

"I don't know *they* are, but I know he killed you. And he's been a big pussy about it since."

"Do you want something to eat? Or would you like to take a walk with me?" Persephone stood again, wringing her hands.

Lexi wanted this to be real, but it was too easy.

You call this easy?

Compared to the past few decades of hiding and having no answers, she did. "I want to know what's going on." If Actaeon were here, he'd tell her. The only person so far who'd been totally honest with her. And she was so furious with him, she didn't know if she'd listen.

Persephone crossed the room and crouched in front of her. She took Lexi's hands in hers.

Lexi should pull away, but the touch was comforting. Familiar and right.

"Alexandra Leia Graham, for more than forty years, I've known this day would come."

Lexi's breath caught at the use of her full name. Something no one but Dad knew, because he'd intentionally left it off her birth certificate.

Persephone continued. "I ran for you. I died for you. Please don't feel guilty about that, and don't blame Actaeon. It was going to happen, no matter what anyone did. But I do ask for one thing in return. Don't let your father out of the Labyrinth."

"I won't." Lexi could think of a lot of reasons to push back, but none of them felt legitimate. She knew—the same way she recognized it in her dreams, despite what logic argued—that this was Persephone. She slid to the floor on her knees and wrapped her arms around her mom. "I'm so glad you found me."

Persephone hugged her tight. "Me too."

Lexi sank into the embrace. It was like Lorelei's song, but real. So much love and hope. "Is Dad here?"

"No. I'm sorry. He never arrived. Without any real management in place, a lot of souls don't make it here. They wander in the void and dissipate before they find their way."

The news soured in Lexi's gut, and an ache squeezed her chest. "So he's gone forever?" When he died, she accepted that, until she realized there was a way to find people who had passed on. This wasn't as painful as losing him a second time, but it was close.

"I'm sorry. I wish it were otherwise." Persephone trailed her fingers through Lexi's hair. Her voice and touch were soothing.

Lexi wanted to sink into this and mourn the loss of one parent, then celebrate finding the other. Her life didn't afford her those luxuries. "Where's Cerberus?"

"He's not your ally." Persephone stiffened, then pushed her back.

He's my destiny. Which was ridiculous, because fate was bullshit. "He got me this far."

"And he'll kill me if he's allowed out."

"He won't." Not after the way he talked about Mom. The reverence… The adoration… It wouldn't happen. "Is he here?"

"Yes."

"Let me see him."

Persephone sighed as she stood, then offered Lexi a hand up. She led Lexi upstairs and paused in front of a door at the end of the hallway.

"Rethink this, please." Persephone's voice was kind and sad.

Lexi grabbed the knob and opened the door. It took a moment for her eyes to adjust to the darkness, but a slowly growing light emanating from the middle of the room helped.

Cerberus in his hound form lay in the middle of the room, surrounded by glowing letters. His front shoulder was bent at an awkward position. He raised one head and met her gaze with a whimper, before dropping his chin back to the ground.

Lexi's heart caved in on itself. "What did you do to him?"

It had been ages since Actaeon did any tracking. Hunting was in his blood, but he didn't have much use for it as a taxi driver, or in the other dozen or so professions he'd held before that.

Today was one of those days he praised his mother for passing on the gift. He followed the scent of Lexi mixed with centaur.

When he reached the River Styx, he was assaulted by too many memories to sift through. Fractured snippets of his past. Las Vegas. Finding

Cassandra's broken body. Coming for her and failing. Lexi recounting her dream.

A boat drifted toward him, the ferryman pushing his oar in the water. There was only one problem. He couldn't afford the fee.

Funny how, in the midst of illusions and gods and tricks and monsters, such a small thing threatened to derail it all.

"Charon," Actaeon said when the boat rested against the shore.

The ferryman wore a cloak with a hood that hid his face, and sleeves that covered his hands. It was difficult to focus on him long enough distinguish more than a vague impression of a shape. "Hero." Even his voice was more of a suggestion than a sound.

"What are the odds I could catch a ride across the river?"

Charon's laugh was raspy. "Can you pay the toll?"

Actaeon made a show of patting his pockets. "Damn. Left my wallet in my other pants." It wasn't as simple as offering a gold coin. The payment required him to sacrifice something he held dear. When he came for Cassandra, he offered a bracelet that his mother had given him, centuries ago. He didn't value anything that much these days. "I don't have anything to offer."

"Yes you do." Charon's certainty was chilling. "And I think you'll pay."

"Any terms?" Actaeon didn't know why he was negotiating. The price would be a favor, and he wasn't owing that debt to anyone. He couldn't afford this toll. Except it was for Lexi.

Lexi.

A pain-in-the-ass woman he'd known less than a week? No. Cassandra said he'd come for her. He'd failed her.

But he hadn't failed Lexi yet.

Charon leaned in, resting his weight on the oar. "If you're looking for the loophole, there isn't one. Making this journey isn't your ticket from life, and dying won't free you from a debt to me."

Actaeon steeled himself and summoned the words. "All right. You can have your favor. Take me across."

CHAPTER SEVENTEEN

Cerberus had dislocated his shoulder, or its ethereal equivalent. He had known his soul could take damage, but the last few days drove home the point. Hard.

His ears perked up at the familiar sound of Lexi's voice. Was he hallucinating? Footsteps followed, and she appeared in the light of the carvings. She ran at him through the bars and knelt at his side.

Because of course the prison was an illusion. He rolled his eyes at himself.

"What happened?" Concern filled her voice, and she cradled one of his heads in her lap. She looked behind her. "Why?"

"This is the way it has to be." Persephone stepped into the dim light.

It was really her. But she wasn't right. The cool tone in her voice… The way she refused to look at him…

"He's loyal to you," Lexi said. She stroked a hand along his jaw. The touch was soothing.

"He's loyal to Hades." Persephone met his gaze, and her expression softened. Was that sadness on her face? It vanished before he could be certain.

Lexi looked at Cerberus. "Tell her that's not true. Tell her what you told me. That she's your queen. That you love her."

He couldn't hear Hades in here, with the spell surrounding him, but this was something he couldn't lie about. "She's right. I serve Hades above all else. I've never made a secret of that."

"Explain this to me," Lexi said to Persephone, pleading. "Why is he locked up?"

"Leave him here, and I will." Any sympathy Persephone had displayed vanished.

He had so much he wanted to talk to Lexi about. What happened in Aphrodite's temple; what was blossoming between them—he didn't even know if he could define that; what had temporarily locked away her memories of Las Vegas...

And none of it was a priority while they were in here.

"I'm not leaving." Lexi's tone was firm and fierce. "Explain it to me now."

Persephone sighed. "Cassandra, the other woman from your last dream, saw the events unfolding now. Has anyone explained to you what you are?"

"Oracle. Sees the truth of things. Special. Blah, blah, blah." Lexi waved impatiently. "Skip the backstory, and I'll ask questions if I get lost along the way."

Persephone clucked. "She saw her death and mine. She saw you with Cerberus and Actaeon—a lot of people did. And she saw you entering the labyrinth. But there are fuzzy parts. Her visions are never fuzzy, except when they involve you. You either free Hades and he kills me and his brothers, and enslaves the world, or you destroy him. So many cogs turned to bring you here. A lot of that was Hades, working through Morpheus and Cerberus, to make sure you arrived. Some of it was us, trying to get you here, instead of to the labyrinth."

Cerberus was sick of fate in a way he never thought possible. The way it wormed into so many random corners of life. The whole *this is your destiny* thing could really fuck with a day.

Lexi's expression shifted through a rainbow of emotions. What was she thinking?

As Persephone described the events leading up to now, he couldn't help but wonder about Actaeon's statement. *Self-fulfilling prophecy.* How much of this would have happened without interference? All of it. Because there was no other way for it to happen. Actaeon was deluding himself if he thought otherwise.

"So the lot of you decided I should come down here and save someone's ass, but not actually me, the two big bruisers you set me up with, and you stuck me in the middle of this clusterfuck to make it happen?" Lexi sounded furious. "Wow. Way to be helpless little babies about the whole thing."

Persephone pursed her lips. Cerberus knew the look. It meant she was tempering irritation with patience. "You're oversimplifying things," she said.

"And you're overcomplicating them." Lexi ran a soothing hand across Cerberus' jaw one more time, before gently moving his head from her lap and standing. "Why do I have to be involved in any of this? Why do they?"

"Because Cassandra saw—"

"I see a lot of things too." Lexi took a step toward her mother. "I see gods killing for their amusement. Demanding worship because their egos were wounded when they didn't get enough tribute. And you dragged me here because… Why again? How do I know Hades will do worse?"

He wouldn't. Cerberus didn't like Persephone trying to poison Lexi's mind. Hades would exact vengeance, but he would be benevolent compared to Poseidon or Zeus.

"I haven't told you everything," Persephone said.

Lexi crossed her arms. "Oh, by all means. Enlighten me. Answer any one of my questions."

"All right. Cerberus and Actaeon came with you because the only thing that's certain is you'll love them both, and they'll love you. I can't see the red strings, but Cassandra can. You can. Your fate is with one of them. I'd like to say both, but I'm sorry child, Cerberus can't leave this place. I wish more than anyone that weren't true, but if he gets free, he'll kill me. Destroy my soul so I'm gone forever. And he'll free Hades."

Cerberus' heart swelled and collapsed in the span of a few beats. It was too much to process. He and Lexi were fated to be together. But killing Persephone? No. Hades wouldn't ask that of him.

Lexi clenched her jaw, to keep a leash on the fury and irritation surging inside. Her entire life she'd been told gods were as close to omnipotent as it got. Sure, they had to obey a few basic laws, but for the most part, if they had enough power, they could make anything happen that they wanted.

And now a mother she had no personal memories of—the lady everyone told her was a pillar of virtue and goodness—was spouting nonsense about Lexi being beholden to some stupid fucking vision about the future.

"Let Cerberus go." Lexi refused to believe he'd do the things Persephone said he would.

And she would *not* be told who she would love. She felt affection for the shifter lying at her feet, but apparently, that was manufactured too. How much of her life had been manufactured to put her in this ridiculous position?

"No," Persephone said. "Come back downstairs and talk to me. Ask questions. Let me help you understand."

"*No.*" Lexi mimicked her tone. "Don't talk to me like I'm a child." She stepped to the line of characters on the floor and scuffed one with the toe of her sneaker. The glow emanating from the symbols flickered.

"*Alexandra Leia Graham.*" Persephone grabbed her wrist and tried to pull her back.

Lexi let bitterness leak into her laugh and yanked from her mother's grasp. She scuffed at more of the letters, until several of them were gone. The darkness in the room vanished, as did the glow. She heard a soft grunt behind her, and looked over her shoulder to see Cerberus in human form, pushing to his knees. His shoulder still didn't look right, and his expression was pained.

Her heart clenched. Because he was a friend and a trusted ally. Not because some random vision determined they should be involved in a twisted romance.

"I wanted to meet you," she said to Persephone. "I was so desperate to find you, this woman who everyone adored. And I just... I don't know what to think. What to say."

"I'm a queen. You will be too. Married to another hero. Held above—"

"Stop. I never want to be held above anyone." Lexi hated the taste of the words. Despised the idea that someone thought they could dictate her future. She held a hand out to Cerberus and staggered when he leaned his weight into her, but found her balance.

"I have to make tough decisions. And I'm not doing this for selfish reasons. Hades has to stay confined."

Lexi scrubbed her face and walked with Cerberus toward the door. She brushed past Persephone. "What if he turns out to be a good guy? People were wrong about you."

"Don't." Cerberus' voice was weak, but the command was enough to stop Lexi.

She looked at him, startled. "What?"

"She's right. From everything I can verify, she's not only telling the truth, but she's also got a good point. Don't write her off because this isn't your world."

The reprimand hurt more than any words from a mother she'd never known. "You can't side with her. She wants to destroy you. Slowly."

"I'm not siding with her. I mean… I guess, in a way, I am. You need to understand the reality of this situation, though. Sometimes fate is simple—a straight line from A to Z. And sometimes it's a complicated fucker." He sounded tired, and she hated that. She wasn't too fond of his words, either. "And she's right."

"She's right that you'll kill her, to free your master?" Lexi couldn't believe what she was hearing.

"I serve Hades. I do what he commands."

She stared at him in disbelief. "What if he commanded you to love me? Is that why there's a red string running between us?"

Cerberus shook his head. "He can't make me feel what I don't feel."

"Yeah. Okay." She dropped his arm and let him lean against the nearby wall. "I'm done here. Your rules are convenient and seem to serve whoever is stating them at the time, and I'm not playing your twisted, fucked-up game of life."

She looked at Persephone. "And don't you dare put him back behind those wards." Not that Lexi had any idea how she'd back up the implied threat, or where she was going, or what she'd do next, but she couldn't listen to this anymore.

She walked down the stairs and out the front door.

CHAPTER EIGHTEEN

Charon pulled the boat up to the other side of the river, and Actaeon stepped ashore.

"Persephone's house is about three blocks north." Charon gestured.

"Great. Thanks."

Charon grinned. "I'll be in touch."

Actaeon was already walking away. "I can't wait."

He strolled along dirt-packed roads, in the direction indicated. Lexi's scent grew stronger, the further he walked.

He never understood why media pre-enlightenment portrayed the underworld as a cavernous land of rock and fire. Souls lived down here. Where each went dictated the shape of the town and the housing, but the underworld was a very real embodiment of urban sprawl, spanning thousands of years of cultures and technologies.

He approached a large yard with a white picket fence. An orchard sat behind the house, and large trees lined the front yard. Persephone had taken a lot of influences from her short time on Earth, post escape.

He strolled up the walk, unsure what to expect. Lexi's scent was strongest here. Every inch of Actaeon coiled with tension, ready for the unexpected.

"Oh hey. Fate dump you here too, or are you in on the scheme?" Lexi's voice drew his attention. She sat on a porch swing, lazily drifting back and forth, a scowl on her face. She didn't look kidnapped, abused, or raped. She just looked pissed off.

"You're all right." He climbed wooden steps that should have creaked, based on their appearance, but didn't.

"I'm irritated as fuck."

They had different definitions of *all right*. "But you're not hurt."

"Only my soul."

He sat next to her, not surprised when she scooted aside to put a couple of inches of space between them. "Let's try this again. One minute you were yelling at me for killing your mother, and the next you were gone, and all traces indicated you were taken by something fierce and dangerous."

"I'm sorry about that. Or rather, I'm sorry you were worried. I didn't have anything to do with it. Did you?"

He glared. "Does it look like it?"

"I don't know anymore. Apparently I didn't know to begin with. But I shouldn't take it out on you."

He was missing so many pieces. "Why are you out here?"

"I'm pissed off at my mother. And Cerberus, but I tried to walk away from him, and I can't. He's hurt. Something inside me won't let me leave." Frustration and anguish filled her voice. "I'm glad you're here though."

That made him feel better than he expected. "Why is that?"

"Lots of reasons. Near the top of the list at the moment is that you've always been honest with me."

Except that one time, or those couple of times, he neglected to mention details about Cassandra. A source-less breeze blew across the yard, scattering lilac petals over the grass.

"You've always been honest with me," Lexi repeated.

He braced himself. This had the potential to turn things ugly. "What do you want to know?"

"Whatever you haven't told me that's making you hesitate? Because, so help me, if you're in on this making-fate-happen thing, I'm going to… I don't know. Make you go back to your invisible death match. Or something."

He shouldn't be amused at her phrasing, but his sense of humor was a bit warped. "You know how I feel about fate—a bunch of bullshit prophecies people breathe life into, to make themselves feel better."

"So what are you hiding?"

Right. The thing that would make him sound like a liar. Might as well get it out of the way now, while she was pissed off anyway. "Before Cassandra died, she told me I'd come for her, and that if I met someone like her, she'd be my key. And I should go with her. So when you told me you'd seen her in a dream—"

"I'm done." Lexi stood, throwing the swing in a wild arc.

Actaeon planted his feet to stop the motion, and grabbed her wrist. "I'm sorry I kept it from you. It's kind of a personal thing."

She yanked her arm from his grip and whirled on him. "It's a cornerstone in this fucked-up conspiracy."

"Tell me what I missed before you yell at me. I'm in the dark."

"Riiiight. You have no idea what's going on."

He raised his eyebrows. "Do I strike you as the kind of guy who gets invited to the *Secret Society of Asshole-Gods* meetings?"

The corners of her mouth twitched, but her scowl returned quickly. "Turns out, your Cassandra saw a lot of things, not just you coming for her."

He listened as Lexi related an intricate tale of meeting Persephone, finding Cerberus trapped in a cage, and learning people had jumped through many hoops, to make Cassandra's visions real.

He couldn't keep the shock from his face, and when she was done, he shook his head for several seconds. "Wow."

"You're going to try to convince me you didn't know any of that?" She leaned against a wooden post.

"Cassandra told me I'd come for her and that she couldn't see what happened after that. That's all she ever told me. Whether or not you believe me is up to you. Did you really leave Cerberus inside, with the same people who locked him behind wards?"

Lexi kicked at the ground. "He took her side. And I told her not to put him back."

Actaeon pinched the bridge of his nose. "Fucking child. They were right about that."

"Hey. I don't know what I'm doing. At least I'm not letting a dead woman dictate how I live."

"You are if you act out of spite, simply because she said you'd do something and you don't want to prove her right." Actaeon winced as he repeated Cerberus' view of servitude. He stood, walked to the front door, and raised his hand to knock.

"What are you doing?"

He glanced over his shoulder at Lexi. "Apologizing to Persephone for killing her, seeing if the puppy is ready to go, and finding Cassandra so I can leave."

Lexi worked her jaw. "Just like that?"

"That's what we came down here for, isn't it?"

She nodded, and he knocked. Her accusations from earlier echoed in his thoughts, asking why he didn't do more. He wanted to point out this was why. Someone always got in the way and fucked up the best of intentions.

Shitty excuse.

Persephone answered, and his guilt surged back, washing away the internal argument.

"Actaeon." She smiled warmly and threw her arms around his neck. "I was hoping it would be you."

He hugged her back, uncertain what to do with the warm reception. Get on with that apology, probably.

She pulled away, cupped his cheeks in her hands, and kissed him on the forehead. "Please don't apologize."

"I—"

"I don't blame you." She looked past him. "Are you coming back in?"

"You tell me. What did Cassandra say I would do?" Lexi's retort was bitter.

Persephone looked at Actaeon. "We got off on the wrong foot. Come in, both of you. Let's try again?"

He glanced at a scowling Lexi, who jammed her hands in her pockets and shrugged.

"We'd love to," Actaeon said.

They entered the farm house, and Persephone led them to the living room. Cerberus sat on the couch, cradling his arm. He was out of place in the middle of comfortable-looking seats and polished-wood tables and shelves.

The scene was chillingly domestic. Unlike stepping into the recreation of Lexi's childhood home, this felt contrived. It cranked Actaeon's tension back up. Nothing about this felt right, given the lead-in.

Or he'd watched too many bad movies in his life.

"I should have done things this way the first time." Persephone lingered at the edge of the room. "Invited you all here the moment I found you, rather than put up the pretenses. Cassandra assured me—"

"Could we go two minutes without blaming this all on a handful of visions?" Lexi asked.

"Of course." Persephone gestured at the sofa and chairs. "Have a seat. Please? I made cookies."

Actaeon sat on the edge of an overstuffed chair, unable to relax. Lexi took a spot on the couch, as far from Cerberus as its width allowed.

Was she that angry?

Persephone returned a moment later with a plate of cookies. "Oatmeal raisin."

Not chocolate chip? Okay, so the setting wasn't *that* perfect.

Lexi's scowl deepened, but she plucked a cookie from the plate. "Did Cassandra tell you they're my favorite?"

Persephone shook her head. "They're mine, so I made assumptions."

Fucked-up family. The thought almost made Actaeon smile, but his tension didn't evaporate.

Persephone offered cookies to Actaeon and Cerberus, who refused, before setting the plate on the table and taking a seat.

"Who else is in the house?" Actaeon tried to keep his tone casual, but failed.

"No one."

Actaeon could still smell the centaur, though not as strongly. There was no hint of Cassandra, though. He should be upset; he was supposed to be here for her. But not finding her was the one thread of relief that flowed inside, and that put him even more on edge.

"I'm sorry for dumping everything on you before," Persephone said to Lexi. "I should have planned what I was going to say, but I was so excited to see you, and I thought the right words would come to me."

"You didn't get a script?" Lexi bit off the question.

Persephone sighed. "I can see what I sounded like, when I think about it. I'm not making a selfish decision. This isn't about *please don't kill me.*" She leaned in and touched Cerberus' knee. "I've never doubted your loyalty. I know who and what you are."

His smile was strained.

This was more awkward than those old reality-TV shows. But still better than dinner with Artemis.

Persephone straightened again. "I'm a key. The last piece of the puzzle keeping Hades locked away. Restraining Cerberus wasn't some short-sighted measure of self-preservation. If I die, Hades goes free. End of story."

"But you don't *know* that he'll kill you. Even though you have this oracle with all the answers." Lexi nibbled on her cookie, almost looking put out that she was enjoying it.

Or Actaeon was looking for drama where there was none. The energy crackling through him said otherwise, and the way Cerberus' expression shifted from exhausted to guarded didn't help.

"Cassandra's visions are typically clear. She sees something or she doesn't." The way Persephone sat with her back straight, a picture of grace and strength, it was easy to see her relation to Lexi. "She describes it as watching a movie, but what she's seen surrounding this—surrounding you—is fractured. More like a movie trailer, where everything is pieced together."

"A movie trailer is meant to be misleading," Lexi said. "As in, scenes that don't belong together, meant to look like they do. How do you know that any of your assumptions are true?"

"There were enough snippets, and she's seen the visions plenty of times. We've been able to determine some things."

Actaeon didn't like the tension radiating from Cerberus, and he had to focus to keep from clenching his fists.

"How do you know she's telling you the truth?" Lexi asked.

Persephone looked at her. "Why wouldn't she?"

"I don't know. Because everyone around here is keeping secrets, and she told Actaeon he'd come for her, but she obviously didn't stick around for that. So she feeds you some spotty version of a vision with *no definite outcome* and everyone does what she says, and she gets her way."

"Hey, now." Actaeon meant to jump to Cassandra's defense, but he lost the argument in the sense of danger lighting up every one of his senses.

CHAPTER NINETEEN

Cerberus' energy returned the moment the circle was broken and his connection to Hades was restored. It was a trickle at first, but a torrent once he stepped from the room.

He wanted to go after Lexi, but Hades made one thing clear above all else. *"You will stay here. Do not chase that woman. Do not leave this house as long as Persephone is in it."*

"Thank you for understanding." Persephone gave Cerberus a sad smile, as he leaned against the hallway wall.

"Of course." The words sounded odd to his ears. He hoped things didn't play out the way he'd told Lexi they could.

He tried to follow Persephone as she headed for the stairs, but he stumbled.

She was by his side again in an instant, wrapping an arm around him. "I didn't think you'd still be weak."

"I'm okay." He didn't want to explain. He'd never been severed from Hades so severely before, and the power flowing back into him was a torrential rain over a desert-cracked landscape. He wasn't weak; he was a kid hopped up on a pot of coffee plus a couple of candy bars and an energy drink. "I hope you're wrong about the killing."

"Me too."

"She's not."

Cerberus' blood ran cold at the assurance from Hades.

They made it back to the living room, and he sat on the couch. "I'll be fine soon," he said. "I need a little time to catch my breath."

"I'm going to have to put you back in the circle." Her voice was tight.

"Not happening."

"I understand." Cerberus made sure to speak aloud as well, to keep her from suspecting he held a second conversation in his head—could he call it a conversation if he wasn't replying?

The air shifted, and the scent of ice drifted toward him. Actaeon.

"Fuck." Hades' confidence wavered. *"It doesn't matter. Nothing had changed."*

Cerberus would rather be doing so many things right now. Pondering the news he was connected to Lexi by fate. Talking to her about it. Now was far from the time—even if she were here instead of sitting on the porch, he'd have to wait—but thinking about it kept him from falling into the pit of the disaster unfurling before him.

Someone knocked, and a moment later, Persephone was talking to Actaeon. The two of them and Lexi returned to the living room.

Cerberus only half-heard the conversation. It would be nice if Lexi were more reasonable about the *you can't change your fate* thing. At least she had two paths to pick from, which was twice as many as most fated people got.

Cerberus didn't want to kill Persephone. He needed Hades to not command it. There had to be another way. A different catalyst. Now that he was were here he could find a new solution. Another couple of days wouldn't matter.

"There's no other way for me to get out." Hades sounded regretful. *"If there were, we would have done it before now."*

"I thought Lexi was important. I can bring her to you. We can think of something else," Cerberus replied.

"Alexandra has done her part."

"I'm the key." Persephone's distinct voice cut into Cerberus' mental conversation.

A chill ran up his spine, and for the first time in his existence, he understood the phrase *someone is walking over my grave.*

"You're being melodramatic." The kindness evaporated from Hades' voice. *"If Alexandra stands in your way, destroy her."*

Cerberus recoiled at the thought, and the callousness behind it. *"She's your daughter."*

"By blood only. You know as well as I do she'll never call me Father.*"*

No. This was wrong. This was bad. Cerberus had to obey, but he could argue that Hades hadn't given the order yet, simply warned that it was coming.

Cerberus grasped for any counter he could think of. *"Actaeon won't let that happen. He'll protect her."*

"Actaeon is a hero without a cause. Defying you would be taking a stand against me. He doesn't take sides."

He would this time. Cerberus had no doubt.

"Then you fall in my name. As long as Persephone dies, the rest doesn't matter."

Cerberus would give his life for his god in a heartbeat. He'd never questioned that. But this was different. This wasn't about sacrifice.

"You're losing sight of the cause." Hades tone warned that his patience was running thin.

"I'm not."

"My brothers have done terrible things to the world. They divided it. Stole people's freedom. I'll restore that, returning the balance between Earth and the underworld. You and I will set right what they've broken."

"I know." Cerberus had always known. So why was doubt setting in? There had to be another way.

"Kill her."

This was it. The order. A command he couldn't refuse. So why wasn't he doing it? *"Now?"*

Lexi was talking to him. What was she saying? She watched him with those clear blue eyes. With the intensity and curiosity that seeped into his soul and made him want to move mountains on her behalf.

"Did I misspeak?" Hades asked. *"Kill Persephone now, so I can be free."*

"I can't."

"Do it, or I'll use you as a vessel and do it myself." Hades' anger shook in Cerberus' head.

Cerberus looked at Lexi. The kind concern on her face. The tilt of her head. *"No."*

"You cannot refuse me. You have no choice. If you sever your ties to me and surrender servitude, you'll be dead in days. Who will protect your prize then?"

Cerberus would sacrifice himself for Lexi without hesitation. He didn't care to think of her as a prize, and he'd made that clear. *"Actaeon."*

"He didn't do such a great job with Cassandra."

Her behavior while Cerberus was imprisoned sent a ripple of fear through him, on Lexi's behalf.

"I'll get free regardless," Hades said. *"And when I do, what I do to Lexi will be far worse than if you kill her for standing in your way. She will suffer unending tortures. Some you can fathom, and others your mind won't let you comprehend. I will flay her,*

have her raped for days on end, and never allow her to die. And when I'm done, I will keep her in the underworld, locked in her memories and knowing they're because of you. Because you didn't save her."

The threat, raw and ugly, clawed its way into Cerberus' thoughts and set up a home. How had he never seen this side of Hades before? Or had he been willfully blind, because he was so intent on serving? This wasn't the god he followed and wasn't one he could continue to serve. Partly because of the threats toward Lexi. *Fated love.* No one got that.

But it was also proof Hades was as warped and twisted as his brothers. Cerberus hadn't signed on for this. Actaeon was right. Hades was a dangerous psychopath with more power than compassion.

"I refuse to serve you. I'm no longer yours." Cerberus dug his fingers into the brand on his chest and ripped it free. Pain spiked through him, and he screamed from the onslaught of pain and weakness. Hades' power drained away in an instant.

Cerberus slumped forward, elbows on his knees, gasping for strength.

Lexi didn't want Actaeon's admonishment to hurt. She was a grown woman and wouldn't sulk like a child. She'd be rational about this, even if doing so threatened Cerberus.

So she was polite on her return to the house. She listened to Persephone's explanation, and found herself agreeing and understanding.

When Persephone talked about being a key, Lexi's retaliated with words, but it didn't stop the fear hammering in her ears.

The air shifted, and her stomach threatened to revolt. Something was going on with Cerberus.

She knelt in front of him, asking what was wrong.

He looked at her but didn't seem to focus.

And then he spoke, but not to her. "I refuse to serve you. I'm no longer yours." He grasped the spot on his chest where his brand sat. The one from Hades.

His scream shattered her soul, and when he drooped, her heart cracked. He finally focused on her and gave a bitter laugh.

"What happened?" she asked. She had some idea, though. His aura was gone. He was mortal. But worse. Even mortals had a little energy running through them. A glimmer. It kept them alive. Cerberus didn't exhibit any traces of power.

He looked past her, to Actaeon, then back to her. "You're right. I won't kill Persephone, and I will never harm you, Lexi. Not to serve any god's will."

An invisible fist squeezed around her chest. That wasn't the promise of someone who'd been ordered to make her fall for him. Sincerity lined his every word. "What happens now?" she asked.

"We take Persephone from here." Cerberus stood and wobbled on his feet before steadying himself. "And we kill Hades before he gets to either of you."

"You're mortal now," Actaeon said. "Worse than having no power. You'll fade and die."

No. The word *die* clenched around Lexi's heart, tightening until it ached. He couldn't.

"Then you'll have to kill him." Cerberus spoke through clenched teeth. "I couldn't have taken him on, anyway. Not in my prime, not ever. If Persephone is the key to keeping him locked up, he won't stop until someone gets close enough to take her out of the picture."

Lexi wished she could be smug. That she could say to her mom, *I told you so*, but the weight of the situation pressed on her. "That's all well and good, but how are we going to get to Hades? We were on our way there to begin with, and this is where we ended up."

"No. We were on our way to free him." Cerberus sounded as though speaking caused him pain. "We needed to be here, to do that."

"So you're saying we should wander around for a while, until the next god or random interference points us in his direction?" Lexi stopped short of saying that was a shitty plan, but it was.

Actaeon clenched his jaw. "No. We're not relying on anyone else for this. I'll head to the center of the labyrinth, where he's imprisoned. He needs a servant or a vessel to get to Persephone, and he doesn't have either. I need to get to him before that changes, and you three need to be as far away from him as possible."

Distance didn't seem to be a factor for Hades. "I'm not staying here," Lexi said.

Cerberus sat straighter, gritting his teeth. "You can't come with us."

"Us?" She choked on her laugh. "You can barely stand. I see through illusions. I'm here to get through the fucking maze. And I still have my hero." It was a cruel thing to say, but this wasn't the time for kindness.

Cerberus scowled.

Besides, she needed to keep him at arm's length. If he even lived long enough for it to matter. A sob tried to force its way out of her, but she swallowed it. She refused to love someone because a random person saw it in a crystal ball. Fortunately, Actaeon would be easy to push aside. He'd probably leave on his own. "I'm sorry"—kindness leaked into her voice without her permission—"but it's true."

"The last oracle Actaeon swore to protect died." Cerberus looked like he was finding his balance.

Actaeon clenched his fist.

"I don't die." Lexi said. "No one saw that. If it's not my fate to die, whatever I choose to do is the right answer." It was flawed logic, since she didn't believe in fate, but she refused to sit here and do nothing. She was in this until the end.

Actaeon sighed. "You can't argue against fate in one breath and for it in the next."

"Why not? You do." She looked at him, waiting for a retort. When she didn't get one, she said, "Mom is the way for Hades to get out. Hide her until Hades is dead. She's the one they're after. She's the one who needs to be kept safe. Please don't lock me in a tower like a maiden waiting for someone else to rescue me."

"I won't forgive myself if you die. I did this to protect you." Cerberus sounded fierce and determined now, despite the strain in his tone.

She winced. "That's sweet. And also some manipulative bullshit. You don't get to guilt me into doing something, because of choices you made. Clock's ticking for you and for all of us. How long until Hades finds a vessel?"

Cerberus shook his head. "I don't know. It has to be someone he can communicate with, who's already here or can get here. Morpheus? Someone else, perhaps. He's got irons in the fire I don't know about."

Actaeon rested a hand on her arm, drawing her attention. "You can go or stay. It's up to you. But Persephone has to be kept out of sight as much as possible. Hidden away from Hades' eye."

"Agreed," Persephone said. "I'm not much use in a fight."

"Where can you go that's safe?" Lexi asked Persephone.

Mom took her hand and led her to the edge of the room. "I don't know what's ahead of you." Persephone's voice softened in tone and volume. "I can tell you have a good head on your shoulders. Your father raised you well, and you have two amazing men at your side."

Lexi still didn't like the idea of being bound to anyone by fate, but she liked what Persephone's words implied even less. It sounded like a goodbye. A long-term one. A permanent one.

"Will you be safe?" she asked.

Persephone nodded and wrapped her in a warm embrace.

Lexi hugged back.

"Upstairs, in the same room Cerberus was in, there's a doorway," Persephone whispered, holding her tight. "It leads to another place. It's safe for me there. You can step through at any time and bring your guardians with you. No one can get through that entrance without you or me."

"We'll catch up with you soon." Lexi swallowed past the lump in her throat.

"I know." Persephone gave her one final squeeze before letting go. Lexi turned away, and Persephone grabbed her wrist and pressed something into her palm. "These will get you back across the river. Charon can't refuse this payment."

Lexi's heart nearly stopped when she saw two wedding rings in her hand. She knew them, because Dad never took his off. "How did you get these?"

"I have ways. You need to go."

Lexi couldn't argue, despite how badly she wanted to remain. She turned to Cerberus. "Are you good to travel?" If they weren't making her stay behind, it would be impossible to ask it of him.

"Yes."

Cerberus and Actaeon joined her, and they walked out the front door. She wanted to turn around and look back. They had things to accomplish. How? She had no idea.

They reached the driveway, silence lingering between them. Actaeon seemed to know which way to head. They were almost a block away when a chill swept over Lexi. It stopped her in her tracks, and Actaeon paused too.

"What is it?" Cerberus asked.

Actaeon grabbed Lexi's wrist. "Don't."

She tried to wrench free. "I have to go back."

"We need to go where she's not."

"Let go." Lexi tugged harder, and Actaeon tightened his grip. Something wasn't right. They were going the wrong way. She didn't know how to explain it any better than, *I just feel it*—the same way she knew Cerberus wouldn't kill Persephone.

"*Lexi.*" Cerberus' voice was sharp.

Actaeon tugged her close and wrapped his arms around her, pinning her own to her sides. "Stop." His breath was hot on her face, and his command made her blood boil.

The air was wrong. It was tainted with something that hadn't been there before. An aura like slime, creeping into her shoes and under her clothes. She squirmed against his grip, but he wasn't letting go.

Something shattered, raining invisible shards of broken glass over her thoughts and knocking her off balance.

Actaeon stumbled too, and she seized the opportunity to run full speed back to the house. This was all wrong. They shouldn't have left. She needed to get back to Persephone. Unless it was already too late.

CHAPTER TWENTY

Actaeon and Cerberus chased Lexi back to the house. The air smelled putrid, like garbage and death. Whatever was in it, it made Actaeon's skin crawl.

They stepped inside and paused. There was no one on the main floor.

"We need to go," he said to Lexi.

She was already sprinting up the stairs.

They reached a room at the top, and the stench threatened to knock him over. Cerberus' screwed up face said he wasn't faring any better. Even without a connection to a god, the hellhound was a shifter, and probably still had access to his heightened sense of smell.

The room blinked from pitch black to blindingly bright, and it took his eyes several seconds to adjust to the change. When they did, he saw Cassandra and Persephone in the middle of the room.

His heart twisted in on itself. She was really here.

She gave him a sweet smile—the one that had haunted his dreams for years after she died. "She missed you." Her voice was soft. "But you didn't come here for her," Cassandra said in Hades' voice. "She didn't believe me until today. Until she realized you were only here for Alexandra. That was when she surrendered to me. Such a wonderful vessel. Unlike some people." She glared at Cerberus.

Hades.

This was surreal. A slow-motion snippet of the past, trapped in glass in the middle of looming doom. He took a step forward.

A dagger appeared in Cassandra's hand, and she pressed it to Persephone's throat.

The dream-like haze that clouded his mind lifted, and the scene returned to full-speed and stifling.

"No." Lexi bolted forward.

Cerberus reached for Lexi.

Actaeon lunged for Cassandra. He was faster than she was. He could stop her.

Persephone said, "Goodbye."

Cassandra drew the dagger across Persephone's throat.

Persephone vanished in a cloud of sparks, and Cassandra blinked out of sight.

Weight, heavy and oppressive and filled with energy, pressed in on Actaeon, and he gasped.

"Mom?" Lexi stumbled and rested a hand on Cerberus to keep herself upright.

Actaeon didn't know if her legs were weak with grief or from the shift in the atmosphere—he assumed caused by Persephone ceasing to exist and Hades taking her place. It was like everything around them—the world—broke. Bled out in a single rush. "We can't stay here." He tried to temper urgency kindness.

"What is this?" Lexi asked. Tears stained her cheeks, and she spoke through clenched teeth.

"Hades. The underworld is his again." Actaeon had been here once, centuries ago, when it was under Hades rule. He thought he remembered the sensation, but his memory grossly understated it.

Cerberus stared blankly at the spot where Persephone had been seconds earlier. "She's really gone. Fully and completely."

Odds where high, if Hades was free, he wasn't here. His influence might be smothering them like a curtain, but he'd probably already returned to Earth. He'd had decades to plot his next steps.

"Do you want to stay?" Actaeon asked the hellhound. "You'll deteriorate slower."

"It might add a day or two to my life." Cerberus looked at him. "And Hades will make those days miserable."

Actaeon rested a hand on Lexi's arm. "Then we need to go. I don't want to be callous, but you'll have to grieve later."

She nodded. "Is there a spot where we can step through the veil and get out?"

"This isn't the labyrinth. The only way in or out is across the river."

She dragged in a shaky breath. "Then let's go."

The stench of rancid power was no better outside the house. The walk back to Styx was silent, and Actaeon saw no reason to interrupt. Recent revelations and events pressed in on him as heavily as Hades' aura—present everywhere now that he'd regained control of this place.

Charon waited at the shore when they arrived, a sneer in place. He shook his head. "Hades is in charge again, and he'd like you to stay here."

"What if we asked nicely?" Cerberus' question dripped with sarcasm.

Charon laughed. "Hmm… No. Offer me something I can't refuse, keeping in mind none of you can afford a favor." He turned a pointed glare on Actaeon. "Especially not a second one."

Lexi clenched her fist and closed her eyes. Her breathing grew quicker. A small whimper escaped her throat. She looked again, then held out her hand. Two wedding rings sat in her palm. "Take us across."

Actaeon didn't recognize them, but he could guess where they'd came from. His heart ached for Lexi, and what she'd lost.

Charon accepted the payment. "Fine. But next time any of you arrives, you're not leaving again."

Actaeon hoped that was countless centuries off.

Rather than take them back to the Labyrinth, Charon deposited them near a thin spot in the veil.

They stepped onto the Hoover Dam, and Actaeon discovered his tension could be cranked several notches higher.

"Of course. Because what better place for fate to dump us, than about half an hour outside of Las Vegas?" Cerberus' sarcasm echoed Actaeon's thoughts.

In the distance, the garishly bright lights reflected off the night sky. Memories that were raw and near the surface clawed their way to the forefront of his mind. He hadn't been back here since The Battle. He wanted to walk in the opposite direction of the glare and not look back.

"We should head into the city." Lexi's voice was strained.

He could say, *Have fun with that*, and let them go. He'd agreed to go into the labyrinth to find Cassandra. That was done. He'd played his part. But he couldn't find the will power he needed to go, if it meant leaving Lexi behind. Or even Cerberus. "Good idea."

"Sounds like a plan." Cerberus looked worse now they were back in their physical bodies.

Actaeon was worried about him making it as far as the highway, let alone all the way into town. He knew how any suggestion that Cerberus stay behind, or simply wait for them to come back, would be received, and he didn't blame the hellhound. Actaeon wouldn't cool his heels here either, if the situation was reversed.

They'd been walking for about twenty minutes, when an old pink Cadillac pulled up next to them. A woman who looked to be in her early fifties leaned over and rolled down the passenger window. "You kids need a ride?"

He bit back a sarcastic laugh at being called *kid* and tried to be subtle about sniffing the air. She smelled human. He glanced at Lexi, who touched the cuff on her ear and shrugged.

He liked that she knew what he was asking without words being exchanged.

"If you're heading into the city, or close, that would be fantastic." Lexi gave her a bright smile.

"Absolutely. Hop on in." The woman pushed the passenger door open.

Actaeon and Cerberus took the back seat. Something to love about these older cars—decent legroom in the back.

"Aphrodite?" Lexi asked as she reached for the rose dangling from the woman's rear-view mirror. The petals were sculpted so they almost looked like seashells, and a pearl sat in the middle.

"Always. Love and praise be."

"Love and praise be," Lexi mimicked the short prayer that followers of Aphrodite recited when meeting.

At least they weren't picked up by an Apollo worshiper. Actaeon had a lot of opinions about his uncle, and few of them were kind.

Lexi chatted with the driver as they rode into town, neither seeming to mind that Actaeon and Cerberus stayed mostly silent. Less than thirty minutes later, the woman stopped in front of a motel next to a strip mall.

They thanked her and climbed from the car.

"Can we repay you somehow?" Actaeon had a few higher end trinkets on him.

"No. In fact"—she grabbed Lexi's hand and pressed a charm into her palm, similar to the one hanging from her mirror—"this should pay for your room for the next couple of days. Love and praise be. And I'm supposed to tell you, *you fucked it up once, and you won't get a third chance.* Whatever that means."

Lexi's smile thinned. "Love and praise be." She stepped back from the car, and it drove away.

If Aphrodite knew they were here, who else did?

They talked to the motel desk clerk, who told them, with their payment, they could have a room for as long as they needed it. It wasn't a big room, but it had two beds and a roll-out cot.

Actaeon didn't plan on sleeping.

Cerberus collapsed on the mattress closest to the door.

Lexi's mask of cheer slipped, leaving a blank slate behind. "I need some air. I need to process. I'll stay within shouting range."

Actaeon nodded but didn't have words. With the silence of the room engulfing them, and the city outside going on as though the world wasn't on the brink of collapse, he struggled to draw breath.

A little time would be good for all of them.

She shouldered her backpack and walked out the door, and he sank into the one chair in the room and dropped his face into his hands. What now?

Lexi's mind whirred a million miles a minute, with only one thought remaining near the surface long enough for her to focus on it. She wanted to run so very far from this. Leave all of it behind, and pretend she was a normal woman, who aged gracefully, and whose worst fear about the gods was that a neighbor might nominate her for sacrifice if she was in the wrong city.

She understood why Actaeon had hidden for so long.

Except she didn't understand. She wanted to. The thrum of grief and frustration that beat against the inside of her skull begged her to see where he was coming from. To leave and never look back.

A strange sound reached her ears. A series of thumps. No… it was more like punches. A boxing gym came into view, and she let a grim smile slip out. She didn't have any idea how to fight—her life was hiding and illusion—but she wanted to beat the shit out of something.

She wandered through the front door, and the scent of chalk and sweat assaulted her. A place like this would suck for Cerberus or Actaeon.

Thinking of Cerberus squeezed tight in her chest, coating her tongue with conflict.

A ring was at the far end of the room, and a couple of heavy bags hung in the opposite corner.

"—help you?" the guy behind the front counter asked.

She reached in her bag. What did she have? Mom's locket slipped into her hand, and she choked on a sob. "How much to hit something for a couple of hours?"

The guy chuckled. "Free. But tape or gloves cost."

"I'm good without. Thanks."

He shrugged. "Your knuckles. Don't bleed on the gear."

She wasn't worried about that. She'd never met a physical surface that could break her skin.

A couple of guys sparred in the ring, but otherwise the gym was empty. Perfect. She secured her bag in a locker, pocketed the key, and turned to the furthest punching bag from the door.

Fists hitting practice mats became her rhythm, as she knocked a few tentative strikes against her target. She'd found and lost Mom twice in just a few hours. The first time due to a difference in opinion, and the second to her own father. Lexi would never have a chance to see if she and Persephone had anything in common. She'd never get to discover what everyone loved about her mother.

Her arms burned from the exertion, but she kept hitting. With each blow against canvas, a new thought piled on top of the previous. Cerberus had given up everything. For her?

That couldn't be right.

Punch.

He was dying.

Punch.

Because fate had a fucked-up sense of self-importance.

Punch.

And Lexi was supposed to love him. She might, if she wasn't so bothered by the idea of someone else dictating her future. Not that it mattered now.

Punch.

He'd soon be dead. Like Mom.

Punch.

The asshole sperm donor who called himself Lexi's father was free.

Punch.

And she was still a helpless little girl.

Punch.

She might as well be twenty and scared and running for her life after Dad's death again.

Punch.

She was that useless.

"Whoa." Actaeon's voice cut through her haze of fury choked by powerlessness. "You're going to kill this poor bag." He grabbed the chain securing it to the ceiling. "Or more likely, you're going to keep throwing weak punches, and it's going to keep mocking you."

She turned a withering gaze on him. He was the last fucking thing she needed. "Go away."

"No."

She tried to make herself turn away. Willed her feet to carry her to the locker, so she could grab her bag, and walk out the door. Herself wasn't listening. "What do you want?"

He worked his jaw. "I was going to tell you Cerberus is worried about you, and to come back, but I'm worried too. Talk to me."

"I don't do talking. Not with you." She had before, though. She wanted to again. To empty her head and get her thoughts out, even if it was just so they'd stop poisoning her. She didn't think she could handle a callous brush-off, though.

"Turn it up," one of the sparring guys shouted.

Lexi winced at the sudden shift in sound, but gave her attention to the TV hanging over the front counter. She didn't know the man on screen, but his face and dark hair looked a lot like hers.

"Good evening, Las Vegas and everyone else watching." His greeting rolled through the room.

The banner at the bottom of the screen said *Hades, Lord of the Underworld, announces fight of the century.*

"That's not really him." She was barely aware she'd spoken aloud.

"That's him." Actaeon's voice was quiet but tense.

Hades continued. "It's come to my attention that my brothers have told most of you I'm dead. I'm so far from it."

Something pressed in on Lexi, suffocating, like what she felt in the underworld. She gasped to breathe through it, but she couldn't.

"And you may be watching and wondering who I am, to make a claim like that. I'll show you." The camera pulled away from him and displayed a series of four traffic cams along the strip.

Shadows glided in, smothering the light. Outside, Lexi saw the same thing reflected in the background.

A chorus of screams spilled through the TV speakers, mingling with the faint horror in here, as if thousands of lives cried out, and were silenced.

And then it stopped, as if someone snapped their fingers. Bodies lay on the street, unmoving. Hundreds. And the camera was back on Hades.

"I know life has been hard the last few decades. Gods demanding tribute. Frequently unreasonably. I haven't been here, but my servants have, and they've showed me the terror you've experienced." He sounded so amenable, for someone who had snuffed out hundreds, maybe thousands of lives.

"I want that to change. I challenge my brothers, Poseidon and Zeus, to meet me face to face. No more hiding behind prisons and heroes. I'll destroy them, and I'll show you all what a real god can do."

The screen blinked to black, and then the football game roared back.

Lexi's legs felt weak, and she swallowed back the bile rising in her throat. She hugged herself, but it didn't chase away the oppressive blanket of foreboding wrapped around her.

CHAPTER TWENTY-ONE

Actaeon watched Lexi's face run the gamut of emotions, none of them pleasant. He reached for her, not knowing what else to do, and she fell into his embrace, resting her forehead against his shoulder.

"This is so fucked up." Her voice was muffled.

"A bit. You can hit me if it'll help."

She let out a strangled noise that might have been a laugh or a sob. "I don't think anything will help. You know what I want to do?"

"What?"

"Find that smug asshole and run him through. I hoped maybe he wasn't so bad. I mean, the gods are jerks, but he's blood, right?" She stepped back to meet Actaeon's gaze. "He's been free for less than an hour, and he just snuffed a portion of the city out because he could. At least Poseidon and Zeus wait for solstice."

Passion and hatred dripped from her words. They sank deep into Actaeon's bones, mingling with her accusations from earlier that he'd withdrawn.

That he made things worse, by hiding from what he was. "What if that was an option?" he asked.

She shook her head. "Right. How'd that work out for you? Besides, I'm nothing." She held out her hand, and a dagger appeared in it. Bright, polished steel shone in the gym light, the grip held tight in her hand.

She swung, and he stepped back, startled, despite knowing she couldn't pierce his skin with a regular knife.

The blade passed through him, leaving a faint tickle in its wake.

"It's all an illusion. Like having choices. Or thinking I have any control over my future. Or—"

He pressed two fingers to her lips, to silence her. She stared back, eyes wide.

"Who says you don't have control over your future?" he asked.

"Everyone. Have you been with us for the past couple of days?" Her frustration was almost tangible. "Aphrodite tried to force us together, to block my memories of what you'd done, because she said we were fated lovers."

"*We*, who?" *Fated mates* didn't exist. The phrase made for good stories, lovely fairytales and myths, but for everything else he'd experienced, that wasn't on the list.

"Me. Cerberus. You. Red thread of fate. And Persephone said the same thing. And that she'd die. And that Cassandra saw so much—"

"She also said Cerberus would kill her," Actaeon said.

"You believe in fate. Or don't you? I can't tell with you. I feel like I don't know anything."

He took the dagger from her, and it vanished. Neat trick. He intertwined their fingers and held her gaze. "I'll tell you want I think about fate—what I learned from Cassandra. It doesn't determine your future. You can't ever think that, no matter what everyone else says."

"Is this some sort of *we're responsible for our own destiny* kind of speech?" she asked sarcastically.

"Not quite. Some things are fixed. I wish I thought otherwise, but I've seen it too many times to discount it. But… fate is a fucking monkey's paw. It doesn't matter what people see or how detailed the visions are. Even for Cassandra, who saw entire moments laid out in vivid, intense detail. There's always a catch, and it's never what it seems.

"You could have the two-hundred-page contract version of your future spelled out, including the fine print, and there will be a loophole caused by an off-screen player, and you'll never see it coming. So maybe there's a red thread. Or two. Or who the fuck knows? And maybe your future is set in stone, or maybe the gods want you to think that so they can keep tossing you around like a tennis ball. Fuck them."

Lexi's smile almost reached her eyes. "You need to teach me that trick."

"What trick?"

"How to make not caring mix so seamlessly with doing something."

He shrugged. "I can teach you how to throw a real punch, instead." It wasn't a solution, but they both needed to burn excess energy, and it would help them reset their minds, so they could work toward actual solutions.

"I'll take it."

He showed her a few basic hits against the bag. Left hook. Upper cut. It was tempting to slide in behind her and make this more intimate. He might, if destruction wasn't looming outside. Or if she didn't have his mind whirring at the idea of a red thread. He didn't like it. There was a catch, like he'd told her.

Cerberus was proof of that. He wouldn't survive more than a couple of days. Actaeon hated that idea. He had a lot more respect for the pup than before they'd headed into the labyrinth.

"I need a moving target," Lexi said, drawing him from the thought. "Something besides the bag."

Actaeon nodded to the now-empty ring. "All right."

They climbed under the ropes.

She swung, and he avoided each hit. She stomped her foot against the mat with a growl. "This isn't helping."

"What do you want me to do?" he asked.

"I don't know. Teach me… something? Make me feel not so useless, for a couple of minutes?"

"I'll try." He wasn't going to hit her. It had nothing to do with the fact she was a girl, and everything to do with the three-thousand years he had on her and having grown up with Heracles as a sparring partner.

She lunged again, he let his dodge lag enough to let her fist clip him without landing solidly. She hissed in frustration and swung. Then a second time. And a third. Her irritation was written on her face.

And in a blink, the dagger was back, and she was driving it toward his throat. Part of him registered it wasn't real, but in this light, instinct kicked in and he ducked away from the blade.

She swept out her foot, kicked him in the ankle, and knocked him off balance. His back slammed into the mat with a *thud*.

She straddled him, self-satisfaction replacing the snarl she'd worn a second earlier. "Yield."

"All right." He smiled. Her weight was warm against him. It was temptation mixed with the desire to do *something*.

He needed an outlet, and fuck if she wasn't a fantastic one. He lifted a hand to pull her to him, but she grabbed his wrist.

He raised his eyebrows. "Is that a *no*?"

"I don't like this fated-mates thing."

"I'm not asking you to be mine for eternity." He searched her eyes. "This isn't anything beyond what it was last time." Was it? No. If there was one thing he excelled at, it was keeping his distance. The truth of the thought tasted bitter.

She let go of him, biting her bottom lip. He knotted his fingers in her hair and pulled her down, nipping along the same swell of tender skin she had. Her soft gasps sank into his skin. The scent of arousal mingled with sweat and chalk, taunting him.

She planted her hands on his chest and pushed away, then rolled off to land on her butt.

He sat up, facing her. "What's wrong?" He kept the question kind, wanting a real answer. There were a lot of things wrong, but something told him this was one he didn't know about.

She wouldn't look at him. "It's about what happened in Aphrodite's temple."

"I don't care about that." He did, though. It was that bond between Lexi and Cerberus that nagged him, but he didn't have a say in that.

She frowned. "It's not like that. It wasn't us. Or rather, it was, but…"

"Tell me. No judgment." He softened his tone.

"There was an influence in there. Aphrodite's, I assume. It was almost like alcohol meets ecstasy. It amplified all the desire and erased my restraint, and I think Cerberus felt the same thing."

The information was a new kind of uncertainty. Actaeon was relieved, in a twisted way, that they weren't so caught up in each other they were willing to let the world pass them by, but he was furious

Aphrodite took their will from them. And that was what she'd done. "I get it. I've been there."

"You have?"

He nodded. It had been ages, and with Aphrodite herself.

"Is there anything you haven't done or had or experienced?" Lexi asked.

This. It was a ridiculous thought. He had no idea what it meant, and he wasn't going to delve into it. "Probably. We should get back. I'll let you use the shower first."

"Okay."

He stood and offered her a hand up. When she was on her feet, he kissed the back of her fingers before letting go. *Where the fuck did that come from*? He wasn't going to delve into it.

The most powerful god currently alive had called out the next two in line, and wouldn't stop there. Cerberus was dying. There were a lot more important things to worry about, than whether or not Actaeon needed to redefine his relationship with Lexi.

They walked back to the motel, swapping banter about the weather and steering as far as possible from anything significant. It was painful, not only because the conversation was trite, but also because impulse wanted him to get to know Lexi.

Why? Because of what she said about fate?

Because I've never met anyone like her.

Not a good reason.

They reached the room and stepped inside.

Lexi gasped and rushed to Cerberus' side. Actaeon hung back, smothering his jealousy with concern. Losing complete access to the ethereal was making things worse. Cerberus' form fluctuated, flickering between human and dog.

His shifter self was separate from his servant's bond, but controlling it required godly energy. Cerberus was cut off from all of that.

What did Lexi see? It had to be more horrible.

The flickering slowed to the occasional blip when Lexi knelt next to him and took his hand.

"What do we do?" she asked.

"I have to find a new god to serve in the next twenty-four to forty-eight hours, whom I could swear loyalty to, and who would take me. So… nothing." Cerberus shook his head. "Stay with me until it's over."

"I will." Lexi scooted to the edge of the bed and stroked his forehead.

Actaeon couldn't watch. He wanted to think it was envy, but he couldn't see Cerberus like this. The hellhound deserved better, for eons of servitude.

"What did I miss?" Cerberus asked.

"It's bad." Lexi's voice was lined with hesitation.

Actaeon knew she was talking about Hades announcement, not the tumble in the boxing ring.

"How bad?" Cerberus propped himself to sit up, resting his back against the board behind him.

Actaeon sat on the other mattress. "Hades called out Poseidon and Zeus. He destroyed thousands to make his point. He's making it the Pay-per-View event of the year and promising to kill them both."

"Ah. And here I thought you meant *actually* bad." Cerberus' chuckle oozed sarcasm.

None of this was right. Actaeon had sat immobile for so many years, he didn't know how to react. Even if he had an idea of what to do next, it might not matter. He watched Cerberus, pale against the brightly-colored comforter.

There had to be something they could do. It was a shame Actaeon never thought to sell his services for a favor. They could sure use something like that right about now.

CHAPTER
TWENTY-TWO

Cerberus sat in bed, keeping half an eye on the TV. Lexi lay next to him, her head on his leg. From her breathing, it sounded like she was drifting in and out of sleep. He trailed his fingers through her hair, trying to appreciate the moment as much as he could.

Actaeon paced. It had been irritating three hours ago—now it was background noise.

Hades' face popped up on the screen. The ads had been running all night. Everything Hades had gleaned from Cerberus, about how media worked here and how the other gods promoted themselves, was on display in a grotesque series of commercials meant to ensure everyone in the world knew Hades was here for vengeance.

The most sickening part of it was, with each new promotional spot, Hades killed more people.

A photo of Lexi appeared on screen, and every muscle in Cerberus' body tensed. "No." He shook her shoulder gently. "Are you watching?"

"Yes." Her reply was strained.

At least they'd found something to make Actaeon stop pacing. He stared at the screen with them.

"This is my daughter." Hades tone was conversational, as if he were sitting across from his audience at the dinner table, rather than randomly killing thousands to make his point. "Lovely girl. Traitorous girl. I'm offering… Let's say ten thousand dollars to the person who brings her to me."

Cerberus clenched his fist.

Lexi sat up, grabbed his free hand, and squeezed.

"But there's more to this," Hades continued. "You see, I can tell you she's in Las Vegas. I'd tell you where she's staying, but she won't be there by the time you arrive."

"We need to go, now." Actaeon said.

Cerberus wrapped a hand around his siren key. "He expects most people are leaving now, and there's more to what he's got to say. We need to hear it all."

Lexi stood and bounced on the balls of her feet. Her gaze was fixed on the screen.

"But before you go running off to find her," Hades said, "you need to know a few more details. This fine young woman can change her appearance at will, so she could be anyone."

Wonderful. He declared *open season* on everyone. A witch-hunt that would turn neighbor against neighbor and brother against sister.

"But there's more." He sounded like an old infomercial. "Don't go dragging your neighbor down to the executioner's block without cause. You have to be sure first."

He was metering out the information in a very specific way, and it made Cerberus grind his teeth. It was meant to leave the important details until last, so people *would* run out and start pointing fingers at each other.

Hades winked at the camera. "Keep in mind the bounty is only valid if I win against at least one brother, but we all know that's going to happen. When it does, the first person to present my daughter to me, will be rewarded."

Cerberus dragged himself to his feet. They needed to leave the moment the spot ended. Lexi grasped his hand, and Actaeon took hers.

"But how can you identify someone who can change her appearance at will? I'm glad you asked. Most importantly, she can only change her looks, not her size and shape. She's five-foot seven and one-hundred thirty pounds. No point in looking at anyone with any other build. Unless they're a little thicker of course. Padding can always be added."

That didn't make anything better.

Hades kept talking. "Cameras and mirrors can see through her carefully crafted illusions, so snap photos of anyone you meet, to make sure. She might be a random stranger on the street, or she could have taken your wife's place in the home. You never know who she is. Don't worry, she's not a fighter. Find her. Bind her. Have her here in Las Vegas after I win."

Someone pounded on the door. Most likely the man who rented them the room or someone else who saw them come in. It was time to go. Cerberus' thoughts stalled.

"What's wrong?" Lexi asked.

"We need to use the nearest ley line. And I can't sense where those are anymore."

"Fuck." Actaeon threw a punch at the wall, stopping short of hitting the plaster.

The pounding increased in volume. *"Hey. I know you're in there."*

Lexi tugged them both back to the bed. "I think I can do this. I hope I can."

Cerberus was about to ask what she meant, when she vanished. So did Actaeon and Cerberus. She was hiding them. He didn't dare breathe.

The electronic lock whirred, and the door flew open. The hotel manager stormed into the room and looked around, bewildered. So much for loyalty to Aphrodite.

Cerberus' pulse hammered in his ears when the man looked directly at them. The pounding grew louder when Cerberus looked past him, and saw their reflections in the glass of the picture hanging on the opposite wall.

The man looked around the room, in the bathroom, out the window, and then cast one last scowl at the bed, before leaving.

The door latched shut, and his footsteps faded away.

Lexi gasped, and they all filtered back into view. "How do we find one of these points? What do I need to look for?" She sounded tired.

"There's one in the basement of the MGM Grand," Actaeon said. "I have a lot of them memorized."

"No one cares who Actaeon and I are." Cerberus was relieved about that. "How long can you hide yourself?"

Lexi shook her head. "I don't know. That's the first time I've ever done it." She faded from sight again. "Did it work?" Her voice came from nowhere.

"You still cast a reflection, but otherwise, yes." Cerberus stared at the blurry image of her in the glass.

"Is it strenuous?" Actaeon asked.

Lexi appeared again. "It was with the two of you. I need more practice. For only me, it's easy. I'm still there, though. I'm invisible, not intangible."

Actaeon headed to the door. "It'll do. Go to New York. This time of day, the gate should be strong there. I'll catch up with you tonight."

"What are you going to do?" Cerberus was concerned. He hated to admit it, but in this state, he was useless to Lexi. He also didn't want her losing one more person in such a short amount of time, and the doubt gnawing inside told him that was a possibility.

"I'm going to kill Hades," Actaeon said.

Lexi pursed her lips. "Just like that?"

"Yes. He's prepping for this fight. He thinks he has the world looking for you. I'm going to pick him off from a distance."

"You don't know where he is." Cerberus hated to point out the obvious.

"No, but I know where he'll be tonight, before the fight with Poseidon." Actaeon summoned his bow. "And I have magic arrows."

Cerberus was impressed with the initiative, but this was a shitty time to take it. A hero's magic was based on the world around them, rather than faith like a god's. So the right hero, wielding their power the right way, could do a lot of damage to a god.

But killing Hades wasn't as simple as Actaeon made it sound. Several arrows might would Death, possibly even cripple him for a lot time, but one shot, and Actaeon would lose his target.

Hades would disappear, or send a distraction, or all of the above. It might not be a suicide mission, but going alone was a bad idea.

Lexi could tell Actaeon wasn't saying something, and she had a feeling it was a big something. "Come to New York with us. Talk this through."

"The longer we wait, the harder this will be to pull off. Lexi, take your puppy. Go. I'll catch up."

She stared him down. "If I tell you *no*, does the condescending tone get harsher? Do you remind me you never needed to be with us? That your part is over? That you don't want any more dead weight? And a list of other hurtful things meant to push us away in a fit of hurt feels?"

"If that's what it takes."

"Stop. Both of you." Cerberus rested his hand on the doorknob. "We're going to New York, and if, at the end of the afternoon, you want to come back here and run this suicide mission, by all means do it."

"It's not really a suicide mission, is it?" Lexi didn't like the thought of that. Correction—she hated it.

Actaeon scowled. "It's not, but fine. If it'll get you out of here faster, let's go."

She decided to take the temporary victory for what it was. She cast the illusion around herself, to appear invisible, and followed her companions down the stairs and out the back door.

She'd spent more of her life trying to blend into the scenery than not, but none of that had prepared her for this. As they strolled down the sidewalk, she had to take care not to jostle anyone, to keep away from anything reflective, and to stick close to Cerberus and Actaeon.

By the time they reached the strip, her brain hurt, her feet ached, and she was pretty sure her soul was throbbing. Cerberus reached a hand behind him, and she squeezed his fingers. The contact was brief but reassuring.

"Are you holding up okay?" he asked.

She wanted to know the same about him, but this wasn't the time to get into it. "Yes."

They reached the hotel. Actaeon and Cerberus walked through the lobby of the MGM Grand and toward the elevators, as if they belonged there. There were too many people in the hotel casino for her reflection to stand out in the mirrors. No one gave them a second glance as they rode down several floors.

The car came to a stop on B3, and the doors slid open. "Second door on the left, behind the dirty sheet bins," Actaeon said.

Lexi didn't dare let the invisibility illusion go. She had no idea what kind of cameras were in the place, though. They made it to a room filled with industrial-sized washing machines, and walked toward the back, where Actaeon indicated.

A soft song filled the air. Barely more than a suggestion. Unlike last time Lexi heard it, there was no ache in her skull. A familiar broom closet appeared in front of them—the one from the coffee shop.

Memories flooded back. It seemed like an eternity ago, but it had been less than a week since the harpy chased them into the corner cafe.

Nausea churned in her gut, carried on flashes of what Cerberus did to the creature and what one of her sisters did to Paul in return.

Lexi swallowed the sick feeling and stepped through the gate. The MGM vanished behind them, replaced with a shelf of cleaning supplies.

Cerberus groaned and stumbled. Lexi knelt next to him, letting the illusion vanish. His breathing was labored, his skin pale. His hound form flickered in and out, before his human shape stabilized.

"We need to go." Urgency filled Actaeon's voice. "Are you good?"

Cerberus nodded and pushed to his feet. The strain that ran through his arm, showing cords of tight muscle, implied the shelf held him upright as much as his legs did.

The door clicked open, and light flooded the room.

"I don't think you're supposed to be— Holy shit." The guy in the coffee-shop apron stared, mouth agape. "You're the girl who was in here the other day. The one Hades wants." He reached for her.

Actaeon stepped between them.

"Don't hurt him." Lexi rested a hand on Actaeon's arm. She wasn't going to be party to the fucked-up witch-hunt Hades started, even if she was the target.

Cerberus clamped a hand on her shoulder, fingers digging in. "Him or you."

"Wow. No fucking way." Apron guy snapped a photo of her, then jabbed at his screen. "I'm going to be rich."

"Ten grand won't buy you a lot. Maybe a decent coffin," Actaeon said.

They needed to push past him. To run. But how long until the next person spotted her? She glanced at Cerberus. How long until he couldn't keep up? The trip through the siren gate seemed to accelerate his deterioration. She couldn't force him through another one.

She didn't know what to do.

CHAPTER TWENTY-THREE

Actaeon saw several ways out of this. All of them involved killing or abandoning someone, or a combination of both. He should walk away. That was what he insisted he did.

But he couldn't. The thought was there, but the desire wasn't. He only had one trick left.

He looked at Lexi as she tried to coax Cerberus to lean on her, then back at the barista, who was telling his friend to, *get your ass down here right now. I'm telling you, that's her.*

Fuck.

Actaeon closed his eyes and opened his soul. He reached out, nudging the currents that ran through this place. Power carried on ley lines, leading back to various sources—some of nature, others born of the gods. And one that stretched to the moon and back.

"Artemis. We ask for asylum." He said the words he'd sworn would never pass his lips.

The air shifted, and he opened his eyes. He, Cerberus, and Lexi stood in a courtyard in front of a house in southern Italy.

"What the…?" Lexi trailed off.

Artemis stepped forward, arms outstretched, and kissed him once on each cheek. He returned the greeting.

"It takes the end of the world for you to visit?" she asked.

Actaeon rolled his eyes. "Hi, Mother. Do you want introductions?"

Artemis shook her head. "The answer to the first request is *no*. And I think I know everyone." She looked at Lexi. "Daughter of Death, I'm Artemis. Pleasure to meet you. And you're with my son. Never would have guessed. You're not bringing Hades down on my doorstep," she warned. She turned to Cerberus. "And you've seen better days. I'm so sorry."

"Why bring us here if you're going to kick us out again?" Actaeon scrubbed his face, not in the mood for small talk or false platitudes.

"I'm not going to kick you out. How rude would that be?" She gestured toward the villa behind her. "You haven't visited in years, and I wanted to see you again. Come on in. I'll make tea. But if anyone comes knocking, I'm not taking sides."

"Wonderful. Like mother like son," Lexi muttered.

Artemis turned a vicious glare on her, and Lexi stepped back. "You need to tone down the lip, young lady. You set Hades free."

"It was fate. It was going to happen regardless." Cerberus' voice cracked.

"Bullshit." Lexi spat. "It was Cassandra allowing Hades to use her. She dealt the final blow."

"Did everyone but me know Hades was alive?" Actaeon was stunned.

Artemis nudged Cerberus toward the house. "Most of the gods did. It took all of us to put him there. And be honest—would you have wanted to know?"

Actaeon should insist that of course he did. But looking back on what he'd done since Cassandra died, since Las Vegas… Lexi was right; he'd withdrawn in the worst possible way. He stood, stuck in the thought, while Artemis led Cerberus inside, promising him the best bed in the house for as long as he could use it.

Lexi paused at the door and turned to face Actaeon. "You coming?"

"Yeah." He followed the group into the house.

The decor was a lot like he remembered. Gold and marble spread in a decedent display. Brightly colored rugs covered patches of floor, and antiques sat on stands and lined the walls. Technology was scattered in the midst of it all. A thermostat. A camera by the front door that showed the porch. A television covering a large portion of a wall in the other room.

"I don't want to lie down," Cerberus said. "It's not going to make the dying happen any slower or less painfully."

The scenario gnawed at Actaeon. Cerberus was rotting away because he took a stand. Undying loyalty until it killed him. For what? Because he believed? Was it worth it?

Artemis gestured toward the living room. "Make yourselves comfortable, then. Maybe beers instead of tea?"

"Or tequila plus Valium," Cerberus said in a joking tone.

"I'll see what I've got." Artemis headed toward the kitchen.

Actaeon didn't like this feeling. It was more uncomfortable than anything Lorelei had dished out. Itched worse than healing from a wound after a fight with Heracles.

It was admitting he wasn't making anything better by refusing to take a stand, and at the same time acknowledging it might be too late to make a difference by changing his mind.

He'd tried to fix things, when he was with Cassandra. That didn't turn out well.

Sometimes it won't. You just give up at that point? The question rocketed in his skull in Lexi's voice.

"You look pale, even for you." Artemis handed him a bottle of beer. "I was joking about not wanting introductions. Alexandra seems nice enough. Come, tell me how you met her."

"She needed a cab." The answer slipped out without effort. He watched Lexi curl up next to Cerberus on one of the sofas in the other room.

"You're still driving?"

"I don't know." It seemed he knew a lot less than he thought.

"All right. Stay here and mope, or whatever you're doing. I'm going to meet the new girl and hope she's around long enough to be more than a notation in the history books." Artemis walked away.

A notation in the history books. That was all so many of them were. Atlas. Prometheus, despite his still being alive. It was what the gods rose up to stop. They wanted to be more than a distant memory.

But most people never got that chance. Did that make them any less important? Of course not.

That was why an all-out war was dangerous.

Thousands die even if you don't fight.

There was Lexi's voice again.

And it led him into a circular argument. He'd insisted for so long that this was the best way to keep people alive. But if he had to be honest with himself—and he'd rather not be—it was simply the best way for him to keep his conscience clear. If he wasn't involved, it was always someone else's fault.

He tried to rattle the thoughts from his head and join everyone in the living room. He halfheartedly participated in the conversation, as Lexi told Artemis stories about her stepfather's comic shop and learning to fight monsters on paper, since she couldn't in real life.

In return, Artemis offered up tales of Actaeon and Heracles trashing vacant countrysides in drunken brawls in their early hundreds. *Mothers.* Wonderful.

Daylight faded to dusk, and Artemis came alive as the moon rose. She was one of the gods who'd been content with the worship of hunters and maidens over the centuries, and didn't demand sacrifice above and beyond. That hadn't stopped her from cashing in, faith-wise, on the rise in publicity.

Cerberus dozed, but Actaeon couldn't sleep. He wanted to go back to Las Vegas. Wanted to finish things with Hades.

It wouldn't be that simple, but he wished it were.

The clock crept up on four in the morning, local time. Not that they'd kept any sort of schedule recently. "Do you want to watch *The Fight*?" Artemis asked.

No.

"Yes," Lexi said. "Might as well see it coming, whatever *it* is."

Artemis turned on the TV in time to catch cameras panning over the Golden Gate Bridge.

Hades stood in the middle of the multi-lane road, posture casual.

Waves crashed around the bridge, choppy and orange in the light of the sun spilling over the western horizon.

A single wave crested taller than the highest cables on the bridge and deposited Poseidon in front of Hades.

"Is it necessary to do things this way?" Poseidon asked.

Hades smiled. If it was possible for vindictiveness to carry through the signal, his did. Shadows swirled around him, then in a blink, sliced through Poseidon, shredding the god of the ocean.

Actaeon felt it, and from Artemis' gasp, he wasn't the only one. Poseidon was dead. His energy no longer part of the world around them.

The camera zoomed in on Hades, whose grin had shifted to soul-devouring. "Brother, Daughter, I'm coming for you next. It's a surprise which one of you is first, unless you come for me."

Cerberus wasn't surprised by the outcome of the so-called battle. There was a reason it had taken most of the pantheon to lock away Hades. Death was his to deal, which made it nearly impossible to put him down.

Cerberus wouldn't have to worry about it much longer. But that didn't stop him from doing so. He was concerned about Lexi.

When Poseidon died and Hades made his proclamation, she stood and walked from the room, expression blank.

He wanted to go after her, but Artemis rested a hand on his arm. "Let her be. Rest," she said.

That was the worst part of this. The weakness. He complied, because it hurt too much to do otherwise.

Actaeon left too, in the other direction. But he hadn't been with them since they arrived, anyway. He was wherever he escaped to in his head that gave him comfort.

Cerberus hated the bitter thought.

"I've always had a lot of respect for you." Artemis' voice drew Cerberus back to the now. "No one has been a more loyal servant over the years, and I hate to see you like this."

"I made my decision." He had a lot of regrets in life, but stepping away from Hades wasn't one of them.

"Why?"

"I didn't agree with him anymore. Not with what he's become or what he required of me."

Artemis' smile was sad. "Hades has always been that way, and you've always known it. Death isn't a consequence when you rule the unliving, so he's never seen it as wrong."

"This is different. There's a madness behind it. Maybe the labyrinth did it to him, or maybe it was there before and I didn't see it, but I hit a moment where I couldn't support it."

"Why do you think we locked him away?" Artemis asked.

He didn't appreciate being chided, but he was used to it. There were things he'd witnessed that no one else did. He didn't question staying loyal for as long as he did. Did he? "You don't agree with the sacrifices. Hades promised to stop them."

"You knew better."

Maybe he did. Maybe he had all along.

"Why did you really turn away from him? What opened your eyes?" She glanced toward the balcony doors Lexi had stepped through. "For the young woman my son is infatuated enough with to ask for help? We both know Actaeon didn't come here for you."

Cerberus gave a dry chuckle. "Persephone said fate binds us to her."

"I can't imagine Actaeon took that well."

"I don't know if he knows."

"Do you love her?" Artemis asked. "You certainly care about her. Orion used to watch me the way you watch her."

"I don't know. I'd like the chance to figure it out, but I don't see that happening." Not with his soul crumbling.

"If I were to take you in, I'd have to know you were loyal."

"I didn't ask you to." Could he, though? There were some of the gods he liked, and Artemis was one of them. But servitude? That was its own level of commitment.

She shrugged. "I might ask you."

"Why would you do that?"

"You're a strong fighter and hunter. Fierce and unwavering. You only break your word for love, and I know what it feels like to lose that."

He liked the sound of the words, and hated the longing in her voice every time she strayed near the topic of Orion. He pitied her loss. "I can't serve someone who sits on the sidelines. Especially not someone capable of fighting."

Artemis nodded, her expression shifting from sad to stern. "I can't do this much longer. Tonight proved it. The structure needs to change, if Hades doesn't kill us all first. I plan to go before Zeus and demand we do things differently. If I do that, will you stand by me? Could you serve me?"

Cerberus didn't know. It would save his life, true, but he couldn't just say the words. He had to mean them.

A loud pounding echoed through the house, coming from the front door, and Artemis pursed her lips. "And I know I told Actaeon *no*, but I do grant you asylum. I don't know that Heracles will take that into consideration, though."

CHAPTER TWENTY-FOUR

Lexi didn't appreciate having her moping interrupted by the muscle-bound asshole standing in the front entryway and scowling at everyone. He and Actaeon traded dagger-like death glares, but not much else.

She recognized Heracles, now that she had her memory back. Champion for Zeus. Careless idiot, who played a part in killing Persephone. They weren't in the maze anymore, and she could see him, so he probably wasn't a figment of Actaeon's imagination.

She should probably be terrified of the walking wall of muscle who stormed into Artemis' home and demanded to see Lexi, but she was trying out this not-giving-a-shit thing, to see if she could make it work.

Besides, Hades had the entire world looking for her. If Zeus' man wanted to take her in front of his god instead, she'd welcome the change in scenery and the lessened threat.

She strode across the foyer and poked him in the shoulder. "Yup. You're real."

Heracles scowled. "Child of Death."

"Lexi." She corrected him. "I'd be impressed you know who I am, but I'm kind of famous."

He nodded at her neck. "You're also wearing his name."

"Right." Her hand flew up to cover the tattoo out of instinct. She missed the days where that was her biggest risk of being identified. "You should know I don't care for you."

"You don't know me."

"That didn't stop you from insinuating yourself into someone else's abode and making demands about me. But I know enough. You kill innocents without hesitation because you're ordered to. Persephone died in Las Vegas because you two had to duke it out in a heavily populated city."

"Casualties happen." Despite the words, his eyes softened. "And I didn't know. I'm sorry."

"Yeah. I've been getting that a lot. At least you own it." She glared at Actaeon.

Actaeon twisted his mouth. "What can we do for you, cousin?"

"You? Nothing. I wouldn't want to ruin your reputation. The young lady? Zeus is requesting a personal audience."

"He couldn't come ask me himself? I'm wounded." Lexi should stop with the sass, but she felt like she was taking action. Impulsive and childish action, but it was better than sitting on the couch, watching her father destroy the world a city at a time. "What if I don't want to go?"

"Uh… Please?"

Lexi was tempted to tell him *yes*. If it meant taking a stand, she was willing to forge temporarily alliances. An invisible force yanked her hand hard enough to send pain jolting to her shoulder, and then the tension went slack.

Cerberus. She ran into the other room to find him half-slumped, half-lying on the couch, eyes closed and breathing heavy. She knelt by his side and grasped his hand. His eyelids flickered, and the corners of his mouth tugged up.

Artemis crouched next to her and touched his arm. "Did you consider what I said?"

What did that mean? Lexi wanted to ask, but she didn't want to strain him further.

"I did." Cerberus nodded.

"What's the verdict?"

"I would be honored to serve you." Cerberus sounded like talking took more energy than he had.

Lexi felt him fading, like a flickering match tossed by the breeze.

Artemis pressed her palm to his chest, right beneath the collarbone, where his brand used to sit.

Hope flared in Lexi. Was Artemis…? Could she save him?

Artemis' aura flickered, wrapping like a cord around her arm and flowing to her hand. It was strength and purity, and almost soothed Lexi's nerves.

Cerberus didn't move.

"It's not working." Artemis glowed brighter.

Lexi prayed to the only god who'd ever answered her. She prayed for all she was worth for Aphrodite to step in and do something.

"I'm sorry. I can't bind you to me." Artemis stood. "I don't know why not."

"Deathbed promises don't mean much if you're not a god of death," Heracles said.

Lexi wanted to punch him in his smug face. But that would probably hurt her more than him, and it meant letting go of Cerberus' hand. "Someone do something," she begged. "Please? I can offer a favor, right? I have to have something I can give." She pulled Persephone's locket out. "This. It's the most valuable thing I have besides him."

Artemis shook her head and stepped back. "It doesn't work that way. I'm sorry."

"Don't be sorry. Fix him. Make the pact, or whatever the fuck it's called." She looked at Actaeon and Heracles. "You two burned Las Vegas to the ground. Prometheus can make gates appear just from being near them. Aphrodite rebuilt an entire town in the middle of a labyrinth. Why can't anyone stop this?" Her voice cracked.

No one would look at her.

She turned back to Cerberus and squeezed his hand. He focused on her. "You can have it all," she said. "Every single ounce of what makes me immortal. All of it."

"I couldn't do that to you." His voice was a whisper.

"Why not, dummy? You're going to make better use of it than I am."

"Even if I wanted to, that's not the way it works."

"Why the fuck not?" She was trying not to scream. Or cry. Or both. She was failing. "We're gods and heroes, and we can't pick one life we want to save? Just one?"

He raised her hand, to kiss the back of her knuckles. "You should be a god," he said. "I'd serve you."

"I don't want to be a god. Self-serving, arrogant fucking assholes who only care about people as long as they have faith." She spat out the words. "And I don't want anyone to serve me. I want you by my side as a partner and a friend, and possibly a lover, as long as there are no temples and spells of influence involved."

"I could do that." His smile was brighter, but his life was almost gone.

She tugged down the collar on his shirt and planted a kiss on the gaping black nothingness that used to be his brand. It was like a void existed in the middle of his chest. His tie to Hades ripped something from him.

She tied the locket to the leather strap around his neck. The one that also held a brilliant rainbow stone. "Please don't leave me." Her voice cracked.

The faint flame vanished, and he slumped over. He was gone.

She clenched her jaw, but she couldn't hold back the tears.

CHAPTER TWENTY-FIVE

Actaeon's mind went numb, and then grief flooded in, mixed with disbelief.

Cerberus was dead. He'd done everything right, based on what he believed. He lived with unwavering loyalty, protected what he loved, and this was the result.

So much for fated love. For making a difference.

The thoughts left a bitter taste in Actaeon's mouth. They were more excuses. More reasons for not stepping up.

He tried to convince himself Cerberus was proof trying didn't matter.

He didn't buy his own crap.

And his heart was breaking for Lexi, who sat next to Cerberus, weeping.

Actaeon couldn't do this anymore. He couldn't sit back and pretend the world was better off—that he was better off—when he did nothing.

He loosened Lexi's grip on Cerberus' hand and tugged her to her feet. She didn't resist. His throat was raw and his chest tight. He pulled her into a hug and let her sob, her tears soaking his shirt.

He hated that the only time she'd gotten to be with Cerberus was under Aphrodite's influence. And he hated that she'd lost something so valuable. That the world had. That any of this happened. That he wondered if he could have stopped it or made it less painful.

Actaeon kept the thoughts to himself. He held Lexi while she cried, glaring at Heracles for having the nerve to look uncomfortable, and grateful to Artemis for her sympathy and efforts.

"I get it," he said to Lexi, his voice hoarse.

The body-wracking shudders turned to hiccups for air, and then sniffles, and she kept her face buried in his chest. He'd give so much to make this right.

Heracles cleared his throat. "I'm sorry to interrupt. You deserve the chance to mourn, but we—you—are on a timer."

"Do you want to wash up?" Artemis asked.

Lexi shook her head. She dragged her sleeve across her face, smudging the tears more than drying them, then kissed Actaeon on the cheek. "Thank you." She turned to face the others, tugging his arms around her.

If that was what it took, if he could be an anchor, it was a start.

"So. Zeus." She sounded exhausted but resolute. "What does he want with me? Bargaining chip? Bait? Sacrifice? Because if so, fuck him."

Heracles shook his head. "None of the above, as far as I know. But he hasn't shared his plans with me."

Lexi gave a short, barking laugh. "Fantastic. We need to bury Cerberus. How does that work? Do we call a coroner?"

"I'll take care of that. I'm sorry there's not more I can do," Artemis said.

Lexi squeezed Actaeon's arm. "Me too. Thank you for trying."

Artemis bowed her head. "I meant what I told Cerberus. I would have been honored."

"Damn straight, you would have been."

Artemis turned to Heracles. "We need everyone. Getting rid of Hades. Making changes once he's gone. No one can sit on the sidelines."

"The other gods' looming destruction is going to make them more likely to hide, not less." Heracles sounded grim. "The prison we locked Hades in didn't last half a century. What do we have to offer, especially after the way he dispatched Poseidon?"

Actaeon had that answer. "Us. You and me."

Heracles looked at him in disbelief. "I think grief is screwing with my hearing. Or your head."

"Ha." Actaeon wasn't amused, but the reaction didn't surprise him. "I mean this. I won't swear loyalty to Zeus, but I'll stand by you." He looked at his mother. "Artemis' champion. Heracles and I will take on Hades."

Cerberus was vaguely aware of… were those voices?

"I'll stand by you. Artemis' champion. Heracles and I will take on Hades." Actaeon. That was definitely his sharp, no-patience tone.

Yup. This was death. Cerberus had been sucked back into the underworld, rather than blinking out of existence.

Well, shit. Eternity was about to suck in the worst possible way.

Power surged through him, similar to what he felt after leaving Persephone's circle, but it bonded with him, rather than overwhelming him. He gasped in shock and forced his eyes open.

It took him a moment to focus and realize he was still in Artemis' living room, with four pairs of eyes on him. Lexi stood with her back to Actaeon, his arms around her, her eyes puffy and rimmed with red.

She let out a strangled cry and broke away, reached Cerberus in a few steps, and threw her arms around his neck. "Holy fuck, you're alive. How are you alive?"

He squeezed her. This felt so natural. "It took after all?" he asked Artemis.

She shook her head. "You're not mine. I can't hear you."

Actaeon crossed the room and politely moved Lexi a few inches to the side. He tugged down the collar of Cerberus' shirt. Cerberus recognized the symbol, even upside down. If he hadn't, Actaeon's sarcastic laugh would have given him a hint.

"What does it say?" Lexi asked.

"Truth. It says I serve truth."

Lexi snorted. "There's no god of truth."

Cerberus brushed her hair from her neck, to see her tattoo had shifted too. He kissed the fresh mark. "You need a mirror."

One appeared in Artemis' hand, and she handed it to him. He held it up, so Lexi could see.

Her eyes grew wide. "But I'm not a god."

"No, you're not," Cerberus said. "You're better than that." She was still Lexi. A hero. A purple and pink flame of fury and beauty. And now he was bound to her. It was incredible.

"Can she do that?" Heracles asked. "Can he really serve her?"

"Just because it's never happened before doesn't mean it's not possible. I've only spent half a day with them, and I don't know how he could serve anyone else." Artemis shook her head as she took the mirror back, and it vanished again.

Cerberus didn't have any arguments with that. He nudged Lexi, and she sat in his lap. The thoughts weren't there, the way they had been with Hades, but there was a current that carried intuition. The rest might come later, but even if it didn't, this was good. Great even. And he felt better than he had in a long time.

"So what are we doing? Because I had a really funky hallucination before I came to. Something about Actaeon standing with Artemis?"

Actaeon shot him a glare. "It was real, puppy. We"—he pointed between himself and Heracles—"are going to kill Hades."

"I like it," Lexi said.

Cerberus was adjusting to the events of the last few minutes, but he agreed it sounded like a solid starting point. One or the other alone, and he'd balk, as he had earlier when Actaeon suggested it, but Heracles and Actaeon together… Game changer.

"Sorry if I'm not sold on the idea." Heracles crossed his arms. He seemed to fill the entire corner of the room. Part of that was size, but as much was presence.

"Why the fuck not?" Actaeon sounded frustrated.

"You've been out of the game for how long, refusing to be affiliated with anyone? And now you're going to hop on Zeus' bandwagon?"

Actaeon rolled his eyes. "Isn't that what everyone wanted? Besides, this isn't about Zeus. He can still go fuck himself, for all I care."

"And that's what I'm talking about. When you say things like that, you don't sound like an ally," Heracles said.

Actaeon's aura flared brighter, and Cerberus winced. A couple of days of not seeing the extra light, and he had to get used to it again. Actaeon matched Heracles's posture. "This isn't a matter of *you're with us or you're against us*. I'm not going to play political games. It's not like I'm going to shoot you in the back once Hades is dead."

"I don't know that."

Lexi leaned back against Cerberus with a groan. "Are they always like this?"

"Frequently." Artemis sounded exasperated.

"If I didn't want to do this, I wouldn't." Actaeon's voice rolled through the marble floors. "But it needs to be done. If you're pushing me away because I won't join your little club, what does that say about you? None of you assholes should be running things, but Hades… That's an all-around bad idea. We—you and I—aren't allies unless you or Zeus see reason. But I won't betray you, and you know it."

Cerberus would vouch for that. He had a lot of iffy opinions about Actaeon, but the guy had a straightforward kind of honor, even when he tried to hide it.

Heracles nodded. "Fine. I do know it. What's the plan?"

"It's not so much a plan, as a mission statement. We kill Hades as quickly as possible, with minimal casualties."

"I can get you in front of him," Lexi said.

Cerberus knew what she had in mind, without hearing the words. He tightened his grip around her. "No."

"I'm with him," Actaeon said. "Hard no."

Heracles looked curious. "How?"

She looked him over. "Maybe not you. You're hard to miss. Though I guess I could make you vanish."

"I'm going to need some details." Heracles relaxed his posture. "What is it you can do?"

Lexi raised her eyebrows and extracted herself from Cerberus' lap. She held her hands out, and a bow very similar to Actaeon's appeared in them.

Heracles looked between her and Actaeon. "You can… No."

She notched an arrow, drew back the string, and let it fly. It buried itself in Heracles's chest.

"I don't feel it." He tried to grab the arrow and it vanished.

"It's an illusion." It should be obvious, but Heracles's confusion indicated otherwise.

Actaeon held up a finger to Lexi. "And you're not going with us."

"I agree with the asshole." Cerberus considered the statement. "The shorter one."

Actaeon didn't look impressed.

"It's real simple," Lexi said. "Hades wants me. You bring me to him. I make you look like not-you, until you're close enough for it to matter. Fewer people for you to go through."

"Will they see our auras?" Heracles asked.

Lexi shook her head.

"Does Hades know you can do this?" Heracles looked more interested than Cerberus cared for.

"I didn't know I could until yesterday. Not on this scale. Before now, I was limited to hair color and skin tone—simple stuff—and the illusions were attached to charms."

"The instant we're in front of him, you vanish and get clear?" Actaeon said.

Lexi shrugged. "Of course."

No. "Absolutely not." Cerberus couldn't believe they were considering taking her in front of Hades for any length of time.

Heracles held up his hand. "I'm voting *yes*."

"Take her with you." Artemis finally spoke. She'd been watching the exchange as if it were a tennis match. "You should both know by now brawn doesn't always win on its own."

"All right." Actaeon relented.

"No." Cerberus was on his feet. He expected a wave of exhaustion, but it had passed. Energy thrummed through him like it was meant to be a part of him. "How am I the only one who thinks this is a bad idea?"

"Because it's your job to think that." Artemis was sympathetic.

"I get it," Actaeon said. "Because if something happens to her, it will be like Cassandra again." He turned a pointed glare on Heracles. "Except it will hurt a fuckton worse. It's her choice, though, and… it's a good plan."

"I'll be fine." Lexi squeezed Cerberus' hand. She didn't sound any more convinced than he felt.

CHAPTER TWENTY-SIX

Lexi's heart hammered in her chest, making it difficult to listen to the conversation. Could anyone else hear it? The faint glow around several of the doormen at the arena said they were heroes, but not strong ones.

That didn't mean they were without gifts. What if they saw through Actaeon's illusion?

"Look, the fucker promised me ten grand on TV. I want to talk to him personally. Because the dickwad is going to pay me." Actaeon wore tight jeans and a mesh T-shirt. The visage she'd wrapped him in had tattoos running up his arms, buzzcut hair, and several piercings.

She was proud of those. Jewelry was a first for her.

The guy they were talking to dialed someone on his phone and stepped aside to converse. Three other people kept a wary eye on Actaeon-as-a-thug and Lexi.

She rolled her shoulders, trying to get comfortable in the ropes that bound her. They agreed those needed to be real, to keep up the image, because she couldn't make the imaginary ones bite into her skin.

Head-guy returned. "All right. Hades will see you."

They followed him through a door. She saw Heracles out of the corner of her eye, working to keep up with them. She could still see him, though he looked fuzzy, so she had to remind herself no one else could.

She could hide his appearance but not his bulk, which meant he couldn't stay beside them. He'd assured her that, if they got close enough, he could follow them in.

Cerberus was here too, and would be her exit to get out safely, when the *big reveal* happened.

She and Actaeon followed Head-guy down a long corridor. It bothered her that Hades had set up his *office* in a public arena. The arrogance behind it crawled under her skin. It was true, everything he'd done to up to this point was arrogant, but this was like the cherry on top.

Their footsteps echoed in time with her racing pulse, and she repeated the plan in her head. It was simple—vanish and run—but she was terrified she'd miss a step.

Actaeon's disguise was the hardest, because of the siren magic. Lexi tried to overwrite it, and hers clashed with his necklace. She had him take the pendant off, and she couldn't mask him completely.

She'd figured out how to weave her illusion into the one he already wore, and the two together did the trick, hiding both his aura and his appearance, while still leaving him visible.

The arena had a table at the far end, and as the three crossed the polished-wood floor, Hades stood. His setup wasn't posh. He had a folding chair and a long table.

It was the fact he'd planted himself in the middle of a basketball court that screamed *pretentious*.

"Do you know how many people I've seen today, claiming to have you?" Hades seemed to be addressing her.

The only thing she'd done to her own appearance was put Hades mark back on her neck. Everyone assured her that her aura hadn't changed, but Artemis looked doubtful, and Lexi was terrified something about what happened with Cerberus would give her away. "Five hundred ninety-seven?" she asked.

"Where's my fuckin' cash?" The edge in Actaeon's voice held a waver, as though he were awed by Hades' presence.

"I'm paying in digital currency, I'm afraid." Hades stepped around his table and met them at the top of the basketball key. He held out his arms, as if expecting a hug. "Alexandra. A pleasure to finally meet you."

"I'd be cliché and tell you the feeling's not mutual, but… Eh, fuck it. Some clichés exist for a reason." Lexi didn't try to hide her sneer. She hoped it covered her terror.

"Your stepfather raised you well. Or not. I wish we could correct that."

Should she drop everything now? Heracles wasn't in place yet. He was at the edge of the court and approaching, though. And Cerberus stood inside a nearby door, watching and waiting.

"You know what?" Hades said. "I want the world to see this glorious reunion. *Cameras.*" He snapped his fingers.

Lexi's gut turned in on itself, as the screens around the stadium blinked to life, exposing Actaeon and Heracles.

She saw Hades' smug expression shift to anger, and she tried to run. He snapped his fingers a second time before she could finish her thought, and her arms jerked above her head, to dangle her about a foot above the ground.

A circle of runes appeared around her. She couldn't hide herself. She couldn't cast any illusions.

Terror and self-loathing raged inside. She was helpless. The maiden, having to wait to be rescued. It didn't matter how much she kicked and twisted; she was stuck.

When she got out of this—*if* she got out of this—she was making Actaeon and Cerberus teach her how to fight.

Please let us get out of this.

Actaeon was tense, but when the screens flared to life, exposing him and Heracles, every muscle in his body coiled until he thought he might snap.

"Zeus sent two champions to fight me and didn't even RSVP? That's hardly fair." Hades sounded unconcerned.

Actaeon wanted to shoot him. He summoned his bow, but like before, it wouldn't be enough. Heracles needed to be in place, so they could deal damage at the same time.

"I wish I had my own hero," Hades said. "Trial by combat, with chosen champions. We could have ourselves a classic fantasy showdown. You're a fan of those, aren't you, Alexandra?"

"Fuck you," Lexi spat.

A shield and broadsword appeared in Heracles's hands, forged from lightning, same as Actaeon's bow was moonlight.

"Oh wait. I *do* have my own champion. Where is he?" Hades turned toward the darkened aisle behind him. "Better than a hero."

Actaeon exchanged a glance with Heracles, who gave a brief nod that he was ready to strike.

The flicker of flame lit up the shadows, forming a staff, and Actaeon gripped his bow tighter. *Prometheus.*

Well, shit.

"You can't hold back," Heracles said as he reached Actaeon.

"I won't." Actaeon had to remember it didn't matter that this was one of his closest friends. Taking a side meant sticking it to Prometheus.

Prometheus jumped through the air, and Actaeon fired an arrow then rolled aside before the staff came down where he'd been standing.

Heracles knocked Prometheus aside and landed on the balls of his feet next to Actaeon. "Focus on Hades. I'll cover you as well as I can," Heracles said.

Actaeon nodded.

Heracles swung, and Prometheus rolled to the side. Watching Prometheus was eerie. The Titan had a blank stare, and his face didn't reflect any emotion. It was almost as though he wasn't home.

Focus on Hades—that was Actaeon's job. He fired an arrow. It struck, but Hades barely flinched.

Heracles attacked. Prometheus countered the blow, and with an effortless twirl, knocked the staff into Actaeon's ankles, then back against Heracles.

Actaeon stumbled, then jumped back, putting more distance between himself and the brawlers. Burning pain whispered in his foot, and he ignored it as he summoned another arrow and let it fly. He followed it with two more in rapid succession. By the third, Hades' grin was fading.

He kept half an eye on the fight. Situational awareness should let him stay on his feet. The other two were evenly matched, but it was brawn and strength versus speed and agility. Heracles swung, Prometheus dodged. Heracles followed through with another blow, Prometheus ducked, pressed Heracles back, then knocked him aside with his staff. It was enough to send Heracles tumbling into Actaeon. They righted themselves quickly, and Heracles circled Prometheus.

The lingering pain of Heracles landing on him still ached in Actaeon's bones. He forced his focus to stay on Hades and notched another arrow. It was only the fifth, but the activity drained him. The moonlight outside helped. Not enough, though. He was used to single-shot kills. When he sparred, he didn't do this.

He struck his mark with the next three shots, and Hades roared when one sank deep. With a wave of his hand, he sent Actaeon flying back into the stadium seats. Actaeon hit the chairs hard, but they weren't imbued with ethereal energy. He was jarred, but not injured further. He could attack from here as easily as from fifteen meters closer.

Heracles pressed his attack. Prometheus blocked and countered. Heracles knocked the staff aside and swung. Prometheus side-stepped, struck, and pushed Heracles back toward Actaeon.

Which meant Actaeon only had a couple of seconds to shoot again before he had to move. Heracles missed, striking the ground with his sword. The building rumbled, but he was already recovering. He backhanded Prometheus with his shield. Prometheus rolled under the blow, raised his foot as he spun, and kicked Heracles back, sending him into Actaeon again.

That hurt. Actaeon needed to give this fight more attention, or he'd wind up with something broken next time Heracles landed on him. He shot Hades again, wincing at the drain on his well of power. But Hades was wavering too. Actaeon gleaned at the other fighters.

Prometheus' stare was empty. Whatever made him functional was keeping him emotionless enough to give him the advantage. Heracles pressed on, his frustration seeping through in a series of thrusts that put Prometheus was on the defensive. He kicked Prometheus in the gut, sending him onto his back, but the Titan sprang to his feet without pause.

Actaeon could use his bow the same way Prometheus did his staff, and he stepped into the fight, swinging. Prometheus' counter left him exposed, and Heracles knocked the staff from his hands. It flew through the air.

Heracles spun, but as he rested his blade at Prometheus' throat, the staff reappeared. This time it held a spear head and was centimeters from Heracles's gut.

Actaeon drew another arrow, cringing at the weakness inside. A dagger formed in Prometheus' free hand, its tip nicking Actaeon's windpipe. The three were locked in place, each waiting for the other to breathe wrong and leave an opening.

CHAPTER TWENTY-SEVEN

Cerberus needed to get to Lexi without showing up on the camera while everyone else's attention was on the fight. He'd gotten close, but if his timing was wrong, he'd distract his allies.

Actaeon was struggling. Considering it was two against one, they were getting their asses kicked. Worse, Actaeon held back. Cerberus has seen him fight, and he was capable of more.

Cerberus' primary concern was Lexi, though.

Her voice echoed in his head. *"I'd be doing better if I wasn't trussed up like some helpless fucking damsel."*

He let a trickle of relief in. He knew that sensation. *"Lexi."*

"Yes. Oh wow. This is weird." She was talking in his head, the way Hades used to.

A torrent of thoughts assaulted him. Half-formed sentences and fragments. Too many to make sense of. *"Slow down."*

Actaeon rolled under another jab from Prometheus and struck up with his bow, using it for a melee assault. Prometheus was knocked aside but landed on his feet and lunged back in.

"Can you hear everything I think?" she asked.

"A lot of it. Treat this like a conversation." He would have preferred they do this before or after a battle for humanity was raging in front of them, but sometimes there wasn't a choice. *"I don't have access to your entire mind. Only send me things you need me to hear."*

"Right."

Actaeon caught a blow to the chest and flew back. He landed less than a foot from Lexi, skidding to a halt before he collided with her.

Wait. If she was in a warding circle, she shouldn't be able to talk to Cerberus.

"I think sweat and blood are smudging the symbols beneath me," she said.

Perfect. *"Can you hide me long enough for me to get to you? No, wait. Cameras."*

"I have a better idea." Her smile was almost audible. *"I need you in your dog form. You'll know when it's time. I'm double glad now that you're wearing that pendant."*

Cerberus wrapped his head around the familiar locket attached to the leather cord that held his siren key, attention fixed on the fight.

Actaeon landed a kick in Prometheus' gut, sending him back several feet, but twisted and clipped his shoulder on Heracles's shield. Prometheus used the fumble to spring in and slam his staff on the side of Actaeon's neck. Heracles countered, driving the hilt of his sword into Prometheus' windpipe, and leaving him gasping and on one knee.

"Now," Lexi said in Cerberus' head.

"My love." Persephone's voice came from next to him. He whirled, startled, to see her walking toward the court. She wasn't on the screens, though.

Cerberus fell into step beside her and padded down the aisle.

"It's not you." Hades' voice was strained. Actaeon's arrows were actually having an impact on him. "You're dead, or I wouldn't be here."

Illusion-Persephone stepped onto the court and kept walking. "Of course it's me. You, of all people, should know death is only a stopping point."

"I wouldn't be with anyone else. You know I've always loved Persephone." Cerberus could play this role. He might say he was made for it.

Hades' doubt shifted to rage. *"Lies."* This wasn't working. "Prometheus, finish this game. Kill them."

According to the screen behind Hades, Prometheus was struggling to stand.

"Seems fair." Persephone shrugged. "Actaeon and Heracles killed me first."

Hades' expression wavered. "You left me. When I needed you most, you ran."

Persephone paused a few feet from the table, near Lexi. Was it intentional? Cerberus didn't care, as long as it was effective.

"You wouldn't be free if it weren't for our daughter." She sounded like Persephone. Cerberus almost believed it. "I'm sorry I wasn't strong enough to end it when they imprisoned you. I couldn't bear the thought of you going through eternity without me."

"*Prometheus.*" Hades looked between the fight and the illusion, but he mostly kept his attention focused on Persephone. "Why can't I see you on the screen?" he asked her. He stalked toward them, stopping less than a foot away.

Shit.

"I'm not here. I'm still in the underworld, waiting for you." Lexi-as-Persephone didn't hesitate with her reply.

On the screen, Cerberus saw Actaeon drawing back his bow and aiming at Prometheus. The energy he sucked in was enough to shift the air.

"I'm not telling you to stop this," Persephone said. "Simply give me a chance to prove I'm worthy to stand by your side again, my husband. My king."

"Lies. You've even got the nerve to adorn my former pet with a fake charm. To mock the gift I gave you." Hades reached for the locket strung around Cerberus's neck and yanked.

He howled in pain. The stench of burning flesh filled the air, and smoke rose from his palm. Hades dropped the jewelry and stumbled. His aura flickered and danced, as if singed. He waved his arm and sliced through Persephone. The illusion vanished. *"Prometheus."* His roar shook the seats.

Prometheus pushed himself to his feet, using the staff for support, then adopted a crouched posture and rushed Actaeon.

Actaeon let his arrow fly past Prometheus, who tackled him, to lodge itself into Hades' chest.

The god looked down at the wound, eyes wide and fury contorting his features, as Heracles severed his head from his neck with his sword.

A wash of power spilled through the room, as Hades' body crumbled into a pile of sand. Lexi fell to the ground, and caught herself on her hands and knees.

Cerberus was by her side in a blink, tugging at the ropes that bound her wrists. "Hades isn't dead. But with that much energy dispelled, he should be out of the running for a while," he said.

"Leave me." She was righting herself and loosening the bindings. "Check on Actaeon."

Cerberus didn't like it, but he turned back to Actaeon, who lay in a tangled heap with Prometheus. Neither one looked good.

Actaeon's head was throbbing. He might grin about a fight like this—he hadn't had a good one in forty years—but like with the last one, too much was at stake.

He felt Hades evaporate. It was similar to when Cassandra killed Persephone, but more potent. That didn't mean the battle was over. Hades would be back. On top of that, Actaeon had no desire to kill Prometheus, but he was running out of options to subdue him.

He pushed his old friend off him and stumbled to his feet. His bow had vanished. Actaeon focused, trying to summon it again. The spark flickered in his mind, but he couldn't grasp enough to make the weapon materialize. He'd poured the last of what he had into the final arrow he shot at Hades. More power than he'd ever exerted in a single go.

Prometheus groaned and rolled onto his knees. "My head." He looked around, eyes clouding with confusion. "She was here."

"No." Actaeon had no idea if *she* was Persephone or someone else. He also didn't know if he should offer Prometheus a hand up or step aside and let Heracles deal a finishing blow.

Heracles limped toward them. He still had his shield, though his sword was gone.

Lexi was all right. Good. Cerberus was crouched, all three heads growling, as if waiting for the cue to pounce on Prometheus.

Prometheus looked between Actaeon and Heracles. "You're not real. Why won't you leave me be?"

Actaeon's heart sank. This was the same rhetoric he heard each time he went to visit his old friend in New York. "I am real. We both are." The assurance wouldn't matter if things played out like every other time.

"You say that, but it's not true." Prometheus backed away, eyes wide as he surveyed the stadium. "Where am I? Where's my wall? The shelter?" He sank to his knees, hugging his head. "Let me out, Morpheus," he screamed into the air. "I don't want to be in this twisted dream."

Why didn't he react this way before the fight? What spell did Hades put him under? Actaeon's gut twisted in on itself—an oddly distinct sensation in the midst of all the aches. His body was healing, though. All three of them were.

"Let me out." Prometheus' cries were haunting.

Zeus appeared next to him. He wore the mantle of god well—holding himself like he owned the room, looking like a living statue with dark hair that curled around his temples, and wearing a suit that cost as much as most people's cars. He rested a hand on Prometheus' head. "I'll send you home. You can rest."

Prometheus vanished.

"Where is he?" Actaeon knew the answer.

"Home. The shelter in New York."

Actaeon would be back there soon, then, to retrieve his old friend. "Nice of you to show up in time to not get your hands dirty."

Zeus smiled. "I trust my champion. He trusts you." He turned his attention to Lexi, studying her for a moment. "Seems you know a thing or two about trust."

"Zeus, right? You look better in the history books. Am I supposed to curtsy or something?" Sarcasm underlined her question.

Actaeon wanted to kiss her, though the urge might not all be related to the snark.

"Something tells me curtsying isn't your thing." Zeus didn't look fazed. "I would like to buy you dinner. Figure out what's up with you and your freshly minted servant."

Actaeon was weary, which meant less patience than normal for whatever games Zeus was playing. "Right. So, we're going to gloss over the fact that one of your brothers is dead, and Hades took hundreds of thousands of lives in the last forty-eight hours."

"Sounds like you covered it nicely. Did you have anything to add?" Zeus asked.

Actaeon clenched his jaw. This was why he hadn't offered Heracles a promise beyond this fight. "I suppose not."

"Fantastic." Zeus turned back to Lexi. "What's this all about, then? Heroes can't go around making deals with servants. Madness would ensue." He turned to Heracles. "You saw it?"

Heracles nodded. "I can't tell you anything except that the dedication is real."

"Huh." Zeus seemed to consider this. "There are things the titans know that they never told us. Things we've assumed. Wouldn't be the first time we've been wrong."

"I'm sorry—what?" Lexi said.

Zeus eyed her. "Did I misspeak?"

"Not a lot of your kind walking around admitting they don't know things."

Zeus' smile thinned. "You're a peach. Is that a *no* on the dinner?"

If Zeus wasn't offering up more insight and was unwilling to discuss what happened— "That's a hard *no*." Lexi wouldn't have a problem with Actaeon answering on everyone's behalf.

"Rain check, then. Where are you headed?"

Actaeon wanted to go home. Actual home. "Greece."

Surprise flitted across Zeus' face, then vanished quickly. "You're done hiding?"

Actaeon's siren stone was broken. He couldn't hide without it. But even if he were willing to pay Lorelei's price, he didn't want the disguise back.

"Yes." From himself and from everyone else.

CHAPTER TWENTY-EIGHT

The stadium vanished along with Zeus and Heracles, and was replaced with the beach in front of Actaeon's home. A surge of longing pulsed inside. It was strange, being back here after so many years. But it was right.

He was grateful Lexi and Cerberus made the trip. He gestured to the beach house. "Home, sweet home. You don't have to stay, of course, but you're welcome. Both of you."

"We don't want to impose," Cerberus said.

"I'd like it if you did." It felt odd, saying those words. Correction—it felt odd meaning them.

"Then it's not technically imposition." Leave it to Lexi, to drill to the heart of the matter.

"No. I suppose not. If you're interested, you can call it *home*."

She studied him through her lashes. "*Home* has an unfamiliar ring to it."

Actaeon couldn't agree more. "I get that. Want to give it a try and see how it goes?"

"Are you sure?" Cerberus wrapped an arm around Lexi's waist, and she leaned into him.

Actaeon was going to need to address that surge of envy at some point. Possibly admit to himself that it was real first. "Do I strike you as the kind of person who does things I don't want to?"

Cerberus chuckled. "Fair enough."

Actaeon led them inside. It wasn't a grand, sweeping home, like most of the gods preferred, but it was bigger than he needed. There were four bedrooms upstairs, and he rarely even used the one. "Do you want your own rooms, or will the loyal puppy sleep at the foot of his master's bed?" He winced at the edge in his question.

Cerberus looked at Lexi, who jammed her hands in her pockets. "I… I don't…"

"I shouldn't have put you on the spot." Actaeon softened his tone. "Nothing is set in stone here. Not the decisions you make today versus tomorrow."

"*Bound by fate* is open to interpretation," Cerberus added.

Lexi pursed her lips. "I'm still not sold on fate controlling my future, but I'm not going to let it drive me to act out of spite, either. If there's love for me—for us—I'd prefer to discover it as it happens, rather than pushing for or against it."

"I don't have an issue with that," Cerberus said.

Actaeon might as well be honest. "I do."

Lexi glared at him. "You're not making this easier."

"I'm competing with the man you bound your soul to." Actaeon didn't know how he was supposed to let that slide. He didn't even know why he was competing, except that the compulsion was there. He was attracted to Lexi; that was certain. He wasn't sure if it was more, but like her, he wanted the chance to find out.

Lexi shrugged. "Maybe it's not a competition."

"Maybe not." He certainly preferred this perspective. "I don't want you to do something you'll regret, and honestly, either or both of you can sleep in a different room every night. Well, for the next three or four days, until you've been through all of them, and then you have to start over. And yes, I'm including mine in that."

"I think I'd rather pick *one*. I like the idea of a place to call my own. But I reserve the right to visit." Playfulness danced in Lexi's eyes.

"Always," Actaeon and Cerberus said at the same time.

This was going to be interesting.

"Thank you. Both of you." She kissed each of them on the cheek. "So which room is mine?"

Lexi stepped into the room across the hall from Actaeon's. It was more spacious than any place she'd stayed, possibly ever. A king-sized bed with an honest-to-goddess canopy sat across from the door, several feet away. Dark stained wood furniture—two chairs, a dresser, a dressing table, and more—decorated the rest of the room.

She dropped her backpack by her feet, trying to ignore the lost feeling sinking into her bones.

"I'll leave you to settle in and clean-up." Cerberus touched her arm. It was a barely-there brush of skin on skin, but it sent a jolt through her that blanketed and soothed her fears.

The feeling was warmth and terror, heartbreaking and stunning. But mostly it was beautiful.

She gasped at the onslaught of emotion. "What was that?"

He dropped his hand, searching her face. "It depends on what you mean. You felt something?"

"You." She wasn't sure how she knew that, but there was no doubt.

"What did it feel like?" His voice was kind.

Safety. Servitude. Possession. "I—I can't describe it and still sound sane."

"I'll help." He cupped her cheek, drawing her gaze, and stroked his thumb over the skin. Another tingle of the sensations spilled through her, but it didn't overwhelm her this time. "It's adoration. Loyalty. Acceptance. Change. Love."

No one could feel that many things at the same time and not go insane. But she did. That and more. She'd never experienced someone else's at the same time. "All at once?"

"All for you."

The terror wasn't his; it was hers. Irrational, but still there. "Will I feel it all the time?" This must be part of the same bond that allowed her to talk to him in the arena.

He frowned. "No. Suppressing it is second nature unless I'm tired."

"I don't mind," she said quickly. "Love?"

"Yes."

"I don't want you to serve me." That probably was the wrong response, but the love of a servant couldn't be the same as that of a partner.

"It's what I do. Literally what I was created for."

She didn't know how to phrase what she was thinking. "Today we walked out there side by side. Or, side by illusion. That's what I want."

"I'll always be by your side."

Not the answer she was looking for. Was that the only reason he was so accepting about her attraction to Actaeon? He had to be? That didn't explain Actaeon's reaction, though. "You have to promise me not to agree without question. It sounds so odd to have to request that, but be my reason and a counter when there are things I don't know."

"Always."

She scowled.

His chuckle wasn't reassuring. He dipped his head and brushed his lips over hers, and a pleasant rush, tinged with his emotions, ran through her. "I'm not agreeing to that because I have to. I promise to temper you. I'm glad that's what you want."

"And Actaeon…" What was she trying to ask?

"He's going to tell you what he thinks, regardless."

She broke away with a sigh. "That's not what I meant."

"I won't take you from him. Or rather, won't try to convince you to leave him."

He put into words what she couldn't. Was it because they shared this bond, or was he that much wiser? "Because he's my destiny too?"

Cerberus shook his head. "Because you have something with him you'll never have with me. I won't force you into his arms, but I won't ask you to not be with him, either. If it happens, I won't fuss."

"Fuss. Such a funny word." She was talking more to process his words than because she had anything to say.

Cerberus closed the few feet between them and tangled his fingers with hers. "I love you dearly. Not because I serve you. The love came first. You're young. I don't expect you to tie yourself to one person when you have centuries ahead of you."

"What about you? When you meet the right person, it doesn't matter how much time has come before or will come after."

"It's been millennia, and I've never met anyone like you. I'll phrase it this way. If I asked you right now to commit to me forever—and I mean monogamous for eternity—could you?"

"No." She wished she could say otherwise, if only because he deserved it.

He raised her hand and kissed her knuckles. "And I'm okay with that."

"But you're willing to give me *forever*. That's what you're implying."

"I'm not implying anything. I'm telling you outright. You and I aren't the same. I'm happy being with you. That's what I want and need, and I'm going to tell you if I don't like the other guy, but I'm not going to bind you to an eternity you're not prepared for. If you're not all right with this…"

She sank onto the mattress. "That should be my line. I *am* okay with it, but I feel like I shouldn't be. As though it's selfish of me to ask."

"I don't see it that way, and these are my feelings we're talking about, so I get the final word."

Lexi couldn't argue with that. Or she could, but they'd beaten this subject down. He was telling her the truth, about all of it. "I don't know what to say. You serve me. You love me. You want me to see other men."

"No." He rested his hand on the back of her neck, and the contact stole her breath. "I'm willing to share you with the right person or people. I'm still going to be picky about it."

She should stop fighting this. The swell in her chest each time he brushed his skin over hers was intoxicating. The emotion flowing between them went both ways. She was scared, but Cerberus was worth it.

Lexi kissed him. "I love you too. I don't know when it happened, but I think it's been building since we started talking online. If there's someone else—Actaeon or anyone—I don't want to think about them tonight. I want you to stay with me. To make me yours."

"Put a hard reset on what happened in the temple?" He nudged her shoulder, helping her lie down, and leaned over her. The heat of his body radiated through their clothing.

This was real. Delicious. Not a bullshit spell woven by Aphrodite. "Reboot the experience." Lexi used the terminology on purpose.

His smirk sank into her soul. The way he kissed down her neck, to the hollow at the base of her throat, added to the feeling. It was physical and emotional and ethereal all at once. "A remake is never as good." His words rumbled through her.

"Bullshit. Ours will be incredible." She threaded her fingers through his hair, memorizing each new texture and the energy that flowed through the contact.

"You're certain of that?" He glided a hand under her shirt and slid his palm up her stomach.

She arched her back into his touch. "More than I've ever been about anything." The words tasted good. She pulled him up, to crush their mouths together.

Her feelings were amplified by his. She needed more. To be closer. She broke away long enough to let him yank her shirt over her head, then tugged his shirt off too.

Without the haze of the temple's compulsion, Lexi could see Cerberus for himself. The definition of muscle. The scars. She traced a pale mark running along his shoulder. "I didn't realize immortals scarred."

"You have a tattoo." He scraped his teeth along the sigil on her neck.

"Which changed on its own, so it's probably not as simple as scars and ink."

He nipped the skin, drawing a gasp from her, then licked along the lingering sting. "We can all be injured. It just takes a little more to do it." He trailed his lips down her chest, to kiss along the top of her breasts.

Cerberus tugged one cup of her bra down and worked her free. He teased a pert nipple with his tongue. *"Do you really want to talk about scars right now?"* His voice filled her head. He sucked on the swollen pink bud, and tremors of pleasure sped through her.

"Not really." She groaned with each new touch, falling deeper into the bond that flowed between them. The way he kneaded her breast and ground his erection against her hip and lavished affection on her

bare skin was tied to their connection. The energy. The emotion.

Words danced in her head, more in fragmented splashes of color and taste, than in sentences, buoyed on by the contact. *Desire. Affection. Taste. Need. Love.* She didn't know if they came from him or her.

Lexi dragged her nails down his back, and the sting glanced along her own skin.

"I want more of you." She was barely aware of forming the sentence, but she wanted to lose herself in Cerberus.

He yanked down her jeans, popping the button and tearing the zipper. Something primal and barely restrained encircled them, cutting off the rest of the world. He slid his fingers between her legs. His touch was rough and hungry.

When he brushed her clit and then coaxed, an unending circle wove between them. His adoration mixed with her growing climax, reflecting and duplicating, like two mirrors facing each other.

Ecstasy swelled inside. Lexi thrust harder into his touch and tumbled into orgasm. She didn't know where she stopped and Cerberus began. She didn't care.

"I need you." His voice was in her head again.

She shoved on his jeans, desperate to get them off.

CHAPTER TWENTY-NINE

Cerberus had never felt anything like this, and that was saying a lot. It was an incredible high. Energy flowed between them. He felt the tingle when she came.

He couldn't get the rest of their clothes off fast enough. More than one thing ripped. It didn't matter. His cock sprung free, eager and rock hard, begging to be buried inside her.

He knelt between her legs. When his skin slid against Lexi's, the feeling whispered across his body.

She gripped his shaft. Her touch was light and teasing, a barely-there hint. It was still too much. He captured her wrist, gripping hard. The feedback loop carried her glee at the rough touch.

Harder. Faster. More. The impulses urged him on. He held her gaze as he thrust inside her.

What they shared in the labyrinth was lukewarm, compared to this. It was a joining, leaving him breathless. Leaving her panting.

He pinned her hands over her head as he leaned in to bite her neck. He felt the sharp pain when she did. She gasped, and she clenched around him.

The intensity was too much. He was drowning and happy about it. *"I can't hold back."*

"I don't want you to. Ever." Her insistence pushed him over the edge.

He grunted as he came, hammering hard. Spilling inside her. The circle encompassing them fed her arousal. He didn't have to guess; he felt the burst when she climaxed again.

It was bold and overwhelming, and they were one. Intertwined. Melded. Never meant to be apart.

The edge faded as their orgasms did, letting the world back in. But as long as Cerberus was touching her, they could stay wrapped in this cloud. He rolled onto the bed and pulled her on top of him.

This was so right, he didn't know how anything else was ever a substitute.

"It seems like this should have been harder to adapt to." Her voice was a salve in his mind.

"It's nice."

"It's amazing," she corrected him.

"The who *helps with that."*

Lexi yawned, and the exhaustion nudged him through a rapidly vanishing high.

"Get some sleep," he said aloud. He adjusted so she lay next to him. "You're safe now, and I'm not going anywhere."

"I know."

Her certainty warmed him to his core. It had been centuries since he wanted to remember a moment so perfectly. He held her close, memorizing everything.

Lexi sat on a blanket on the beach behind Actaeon's house. She was leaned back against Cerberus, and her legs were on Actaeon's lap. Letting things happen as they did, when it came to this relationship, felt good.

Defining what she had with Cerberus helped.

"How do you think it goes from here?" she asked. "Like, what are the odds Zeus and Artemis and all the other gods meet up and decide they acted harshly? That thanks to this Hades bullshit, they'll see human sacrifice in their name isn't the best way to go, and ease up?"

Actaeon looked past her, and he and Cerberus laughed. She supposed that was better than sinking into despair over it. They could take a night off from that.

"This is how it will play out." Cerberus draped an arm over her shoulder. "Zeus will hold this summit—or whatever you want to call it—at Artemis' request. He'll tell everyone they need to make an effort to appear more personable to their followers. Play nice on camera for a while and show the world they're not Hades. They'll ramp things back up slowly, as people become complacent, and five or ten years down the line, sacrifices will be bigger than ever."

She let out a slow breath. "Wow. You're more jaded than he is. Also, that sucks, because I don't doubt it for a second. Can't we do something about it?"

"Like what?" Cerberus asked.

"We could wage war on the gods." They'd taken one on and survived, and he was supposedly the baddest of the bunch. Of course, he wasn't gone, but *significantly weaker* was a good jumping-off point.

Actaeon pursed his lips. "I like the sound of that. However, as much as I enjoy working with the two of you—"

Cerberus snorted.

Actaeon raised an eyebrow. "If I didn't, you wouldn't be here."

"Be nice." Lexi swatted Cerberus's leg. "He let me get snot on his shirt when I thought you were dead." The idea of taking on the gods deserved a more serious tone, but she needed to cling to this levity, or she'd drown in despair.

"Okay. Because that makes him come across as more sincere when there's a *but* attached to his sentence." Cerberus didn't sound convinced.

"Which I'd explain if you'd let me," Actaeon said. "It's going to take more than the three of us to wage war on the gods. We had Heracles today, and he's not going to side with us against Zeus."

"So we'll find more." It wasn't that easy, but it was the answer.

"How?" Actaeon asked. "And don't tell me, *fate will find a way.*"

"No. *We* will. I assume, between the two of you, you know everyone. You'll be talent recruitment, and I'll be the sassy, witty brains of the operation." Laughing about this was much better than admitting the three of them were discussing overthrowing a dangerous and vindictive pantheon of rulers.

"I can live with that." Cerberus nuzzled her ear. *"And I'll even let it slide that there are eerie parallels in here to superhero movies."*

Lexi smirked. *"Are you casting me as Wonder Woman or Black Widow?"*

"As yourself. They've got nothing on you."

Actaeon cleared his throat. "For those of you not in the know, it's bad enough to be in the room while a servant is doing that with a remote god, but when you're both here…"

Lexi flushed. "It's rude. I'm sorry."

"Excuse me." A female voice interrupted the conversation.

Lexi's laugh died, and ice ran through her veins before she registered she knew who that was. *Cassandra.*

Lexi was on her feet in an instant. Her companions did the same.

"You've got some nerve," Cerberus growled.

Cassandra looked at him, eyebrows tugged together and blankness in her eyes. "Do I know you?"

"Really." Lexi didn't try to hide her disbelief. The problem was Cassandra didn't look as though she was lying.

"What are you doing here?" Actaeon stepped forward, angling himself so he was half between her and Lexi.

Cassandra shook her head. "I don't know. I was…" She frowned and pressed her hand to her forehead. "I can't remember. I was here. I don't know how I got here, but I started walking, and I found the three of you. Do you know me?" Fear leaked into her voice.

Lexi refused to feel sympathy for her after everything she was both directly and indirectly responsible for. "You don't remember anything else at all?"

"Nothing."

"She's telling the truth." Cerberus spoke in her head.

"Seems like it." Lexi wondered how long that would last, though. "I do know you. Your name is Cassandra. Supposedly you see the future. You fucked with my life. You killed my mother. And you traumatized my friends."

Cassandra's bottom lip quivered. "I don't know what you're talking about. I couldn't kill anyone. How horrible." She sobbed. "I just want to know where I am."

THE END